The House on Swiss Avenue

HISTORICAL FICTION

Irene Sandell

Double Mountain Press

OTHER BOOKS BY
IRENE SANDELL

In A Fevered Land

Lon Prather and his cousin Emory Campbell are determined to escape the drought and financial ruin of cotton farming during the Great Depression. They follow promises of money and adventure to the oil field towns of Wink, Kilgore, and Odessa.

Their quest leads them to the boisterous life of the Texas boomtowns where they find love and hatred, hope and regret, failure and success.

River of the Arms of God

Kate Walters believes she is escaping her controlling father for the life of her dreams when she hastily marries Colby Walters and moves to his ranching empire, Pantera. But she soon finds that the wide open lands of West Texas hold a host of their own secrets that hold her captive.

Only when she is shown the strength to stand on her own by Sarah Graham, a young woman who lived along the Butterfield State route and walked the same ground 100 years before, does Kathryn find true freedom. The life lessons that both women learn lead them on journeys that reach across the years and span the continent.

Copyright

Library of Congress Control Number
2012935168
ISBN 978-1-4826-1034-5

**Sandell, Irene (2013). The House on Swiss Avenue.
Historical Fiction.**

Book layout by Alan McCuller/www.mc2graphics.com

Dedication

*To my family for their belief and encouragement,
and especially to my own Robyn*

Dallas 1863

Paul Henri took the position for the money. With six mouths to feed, of course he took the job. If he had not been so stubborn; not clung to the colony for so long, he might have gone to Dallas with his friend Henry Boll, who bought a farm there. He might have opened a jewelry shop like Jacob Knapfli, or a print shop, or even a blacksmith shop to make tools. But he had stayed with his vegetable garden and livestock, unwilling to uproot his family again; until the war started, and all the skilled jobs like his were gone. So, when Argyle Tucker and his father came looking for an engraver for their weapons factory, he took the job.

But not just for the money, he reassured himself. There was a sense of patriotism also. As his son pointed out; this was their new country now— America—Texas. They should be a part of its struggle. So even though Paul Henri had brought his family halfway round the

1

world to find freedom and peace, to find brotherhood and equality without the class divisions and limitations of France, he took up the Confederate cause and accepted the job. His boy had set both of their paths when he enlisted at the earliest call to war and marched away, eager, he said, to defend their right to rule Texas as Texans chose. Even when that meant he also fought for the slavery of men.

Paul Henri found it hard to reconcile the goals of the Confederacy with his beliefs in freedom and equality that had drawn him to La Reunion here on the Trinity River. Found it hard to direct the labor of the Tuckers' slave, Zebediah, knowing that by doing so, he was denying one of his basic moral beliefs. But William, his only son, was in the fight. He could not sit by and ignore that fact. And besides, he loved his new land. He could never go back to France. His honor dictated that he support his new country. He took the job.

He also took the job, he knew, for pride; pride in his skill as an engraver. He was never a farmer. He found no fulfillment in it. He had trained in the best schools in Europe to ply his craft; taken great pleasure in his skill. So when the chance to work for the Tuckers in Lancaster came, he eagerly took it. He took the job for all these reasons. He took it, and then he wondered what price he would have to pay.

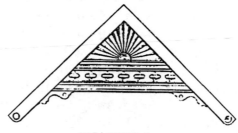

CHAPTER 1

Dallas 2007

When Robyn Merrill turned in at the half-hidden driveway that morning, it was a snap decision. She was not ordinarily an impulsive person, but the narrow lane through the huge ligustrum hedge had been her only escape route, she would reason later—a way out of the traffic jam on Swiss Avenue.

She had seen the tiny tin "Rooms for Rent" sign almost hidden by the hedge just after yet again slamming on her brakes to avoid hitting the car in front of her. Robyn strained to see over the tangle of traffic. There must have been an accident somewhere. It looked like gridlock for blocks. On impulse, she checked her mirrors, saw a space, and turned down the lane. But now, facing the imposing old two story house at the end of the ribbon of gravel in front of her car, she had second thoughts.

Ok, so maybe just a little too "Bates Motel" here.

Robyn shifted to reverse and craned her head around to see behind the car. But a blur of colors rushed by on the street beyond the hedge opening. She was trapped. Backing out on Swiss Avenue was out of the question. She turned back to study the house before her.

It was half hidden behind high greenery that had long ago outgrown the right to be called bushes. Huge hawthorns reached to the veranda railing that wrapped across the full front of the house like a Victorian lady with long skirts clustered about her. There was an aura of past grandeur about the place; a feeling of genteel poverty, and not so threatening after all. It made her think of home, actually. Robyn eased her car forward. She would just follow the drive and turn around by the front door. She would be gone in an instant. The people inside would never even notice her.

But she didn't. She edged slowly up to a small gravel parking area and paused to look for a house number. This place didn't match any description she had read in the rental listings. Still, she had seen the sign, and she had found nothing that looked this interesting anywhere else.

After only a moment's hesitation, she cut the engine and opened the car door. Instantly she was engulfed in the quiet. The traffic beyond the hedge was only a whispered monotony. Around her, birds fluttered and called, and a breeze rustled the huge trees that graced the lawn. The mild January day felt more like Spring than Winter. A smile crossed her lips. Mother would be quick to point out the irony of this place. She had traveled a long way only to wind up in a house like the one she had left behind.

She slipped her purse strap over her shoulder and closed the car door with a thud that was quickly soaked up in the quiet. It wouldn't hurt to ask. The worst the people could say would be no.

The veranda was vacant except for several wooden rockers clustered at the far corner of the porch, a lace of fallen leaves braided around their base. She climbed the front steps and searched the doorway for a bell, but found none.

Making a fist, Robyn took a couple of practice motions and then knocked on the frame of the screen door. No sound came from inside. She knocked again with more confidence, but still met silence. Robyn looked around the porch as if she expected help from some quarter. She was a person who, once committed to something, did not give up easily. She squinted her eyes trying to see movement behind the lace curtain in the door glass, but was met only by her own reflection. Her hair had gone flat again. Robyn reached up to brush it back with a frustrated motion.

Then a sound caught her ear; a door closing probably, and soft tapping of footsteps. The lace curtain on the glass was pushed aside and the face of an elderly woman replaced Robyn's reflection as though she had suddenly aged by fifty years or so. They studied one another for a moment.

"Good morning." Robyn pitched her voice just slightly, in case the beveled glass between them might keep her from being heard.

"Yes?"

"I saw your sign." Robyn gestured toward the street.

The woman's face knitted into a slight frown.

"Your sign," Robyn repeated. "Rooms for Rent."

"Are you from Penrow? I've already told those people how I feel."

Robyn hesitated, trying to decipher the woman's response. "No, I'm interested in the rooms. Do you have rooms for rent?"

The woman studied her with a guarded gaze, her

head thrown back to use the lower part of her bifocals. "You're not from Penrow?"

"No..., no, I've only just moved here from Atlanta, and I'm trying to find a place to live." She paused trying to think what to say next. "I saw your sign," she added feebly.

The curtain dropped, and for an instant Robyn thought the woman was gone. Then she heard the lock, and the door opened part way.

"Texas?" The woman asked through the screen door.

"Pardon me?"

"Is that Atlanta, Texas?"

"No, Georgia. Atlanta, Georgia."

"There is an Atlanta, Texas, also, you know."

"No, I..., I didn't realize that." This was not going well.

"Are you alone?"

"Yes." Robyn hesitated, not sure if the woman meant now or always. She tried to answer both questions. "Yes, I'll be the only one. I'm alone."

"Your mother must be very worried about you."

Robyn smiled when she realized the woman's train of thought. "Yes, she is, as a matter of fact."

"Well, I'm sorry you were misled, young lady, but there is no room. I should have removed that sign long ago."

"I see." The disappointment had to show in her voice. Robyn suddenly wanted this place very badly. "Well, I'm sorry to bother you." She stepped back. "It is a lovely old place though."

The woman's expression softened a little. "You like old houses, then?"

"Yes, it's my field. I'm an architect with Barton & Ramsey, and I specialize in historic preservation."

6

"I see," The woman still studied her as though she wanted to remember her for identification. "And none of these new housing developments interest you?"

"Oh they're beautiful, but expensive! I'm just starting out" Robyn smiled and rolled her eyes, taking a stab at charm. "You wouldn't reconsider, then?"

The woman shook her head quickly. "No dear, I was much younger when I put that sign out. I don't need the disruption now." She returned the smile.

So much for charm. "Well, thanks for talking to me." Robyn backed away.

"Good day." And the door closed.

Robyn glanced around the veranda, feeling very foolish and rejected. She retreated to her car and maneuvered a tight turn in the narrow driveway to point toward the street.

A cream-colored Mercedes turned in through the hedge blocking her path. She waited while it came up the lane and turned into the parking area. A stocky man in a tan business suit and a loud stylish tie climbed out. Lawyer, she thought. He stood by his car and appraised her with a suspicious eye, no smile, no nod. She smiled in self-defense, feeling like a vagrant, and drove out the lane. She could see the man in her side mirror, staring after her like a guard dog. So much for friendly Texans. She eased the nose of her car out beyond the hedge, saw her chance and scooted into traffic, feeling very disappointed and not a bit interested in more apartment hunting today.

CHAPTER 2

Addy Sinclair glanced at the hall clock as she stepped away from the door. 10:15. Edwin would be here any minute. She was flustered now. She would have to calm herself down, direct her thoughts. That young woman had been an unnecessary interruption. She went back to the kitchen to finish preparing the coffee.

Well, never mind. The girl was gone in good time. At least it hadn't been Edwin showing up early. Was that a car door?

She looked at the stove clock. 10:18. What a bother! She picked up the tray and carried it across the hall to the parlor. Before she had settled it on the coffee table, a knock sounded. She stood up and took a deep breath to compose herself, squared her shoulders, and went to the door.

Edwin Sinclair Bennett, all starched and proper, impatient as ever, was holding the screen ajar when she opened the door. "Good morning, Auntie."

"Good morning, Edwin. You're early."

He glanced at his watch as he brushed past her into the entry hall. "Ten minutes." He surveyed the hall like a landlord; then turned his attention on Addy. "Where's Gladys today?"

"She's gone to her sister's. Someone's birthday, I think."

"You had a visitor."

"Yes." Addy stepped past him and crossed the hall. "I've set up coffee in the parlor. I hope that's all right."

"Yes, fine, fine," He followed her. "What did that woman want?"

"Hmm?" Addy settled herself on the rosewood and velvet sofa by the tray.

"What did she want?" Edwin looked around at the collection of chairs. None looked too comfortable for a man of his size, and she had already taken the sofa. He chose a wooden arm chair closest to the coffee tray and sat down gingerly. Too small. He crossed his legs, shifted his weight and crossed them again.

"Are you comfortable?" Addy asked.

"Fine, fine." He reached to take the cup she offered. "What did that woman want?"

"Sugar?"

"No, black, thank you." He waited for an answer, then repeated. "What did the woman want?"

Addy stirred her coffee and took a sip. It was just right. She sat the cup down and reached to offer Edwin a plate of muffins. "How are Marla and the children?"

"Fine, they are fine. Growing up, you know."

"You need to bring them by sometime. I haven't seen the little one since his christening."

"Yes, I guess that's right." Edwin took a muffin and balanced it on the edge of his saucer. "That woman,

9

Auntie. What did she want?"

"She was house hunting."

"House hunting? Was she a real estate dealer?" He sat forward in his chair. "Don't talk to them, Auntie. I've warned you before. Let my firm do the talking. What did she say?'

"Is this what you came to discuss today?" Addy took another sip of coffee, eyeing him over the rim of her cup.

"No," he glanced at his watch again. "You're right. I don't have long. I've got a meeting downtown at eleven thirty." He took a deep breath as if centering his thoughts. "Have you thought any more about the offer, Auntie?'

"Edwin, you know very well I despise that word, Auntie. Make it Addy, or even Aunt Addy, but please do not persist in calling me Auntie."

"I'm sorry, you're quite right, Aunt Addy." Edwin held up his hand to stop her reproach. "But the important point here is, have you considered the offer?"

"Yes and no."

"Now what... !" Edwin stopped short and softened his tone. "What exactly does that mean, yes and no?" He sat his cup and saucer down with an abrupt rattle.

"Yes, I've considered the offer, and no, I'm not interested."

Edwin let out a breath in disgust. "Addy, listen."

No, you listen, young man! I do not want to sell. No matter how many times or ways you, or anyone else, present the idea. I do not want to sell!"

"Addy," Edwin raised both hands as if he were about to measure something a foot long. He paused for effect. "This house, this property is too valuable to remain anonymous. There will be offers. It is inevitable that this land will be developed ..."

"Not while I'm here!"

"No, no, of course not. No one wants to destroy this place around you, Aunt Addy, but you must be practical."

"And by practical, you mean that I should sell, give up my home." Addy's voice rose to cut him off. "I've lived in this house for ninety years, Edwin. Ninety! My father and mother, my grandparents, my great-grandparents lived here."

Edwin let out a sigh of exasperation.

"Where would I go? Tell me that." She pursed her lips. "Where would I go?"

"Auntie, ah ... AUNT Addy, no one, least of all me, wants to move you if you don't want to be moved, ..."

I don't!"

"... but look around." He motioned toward the street. "It will happen. You're surrounded by city here. The freeway is only a mile away, and every other landowner has sold.. This twenty acre patch, that's it. My God, do you realize the value ... ?"

"Do not curse in my house, young man!"

"I'm sorry," Edwin swallowed and breathed deeply. "The value of this twenty acre tract is going to set a record for Dallas real estate. Everyone, everyone wants this land, Addy. The point is that we need to negotiate from strength. My law firm can design a contract ..."

"I already have a will."

"No, this would be a contract, Aunt Addy, stating that no one, nothing can touch this property as long as we say so, but in the meantime we will lock in our price and ..."

"We?"

The word stopped Edwin cold. "Yes, we, I'm your only relative, remember. Your cousin's grandson. I'm it. The last of the great line of Boll, as they say."

Edwin stood suddenly and his napkin fell to the floor. "Listen, do you think anyone out there cares? You should get out more, Auntie. The name Boll doesn't carry much weight anymore. And Sinclair!" He waved an arm toward the oil painting over the mantle. "No one has heard of him since, what was it, 1944?"

"My husband was a war hero." Addy stiffened. Her heart was racing. She raised a hand to her throat. "He gave his life for this country. He ..."

"Listen to yourself, Addy." Edwin was almost shouting. "Just listen?"

Addy stopped in mid sentence.

"Just listen ..." Edwin's voice went low and even again. "The truth is, time passes. People forget. Your husband, hero that he was, is gone; over sixty years now, and while you choose to remember, to deify ..."

Addy started to protest, but Edwin stopped her with a hand motion. "... to deify his memory. To revere this house as a shrine to him and to your parents and all your ancestors before them, the truth is, you are alone. I'm the only one who gives a ... , who cares what happens here. Me. And regardless of what you think, I am concerned about you."

"And this concern you have ... " Addy's voice was shaky but strong, "requires that I sell my house, or turn it over to you. Is that right?'

Edwin nodded slowly.

"And in the long run, what happens to my house?"

"This is an old house, Addy. No matter what you see when you look at it, it's still just an old house. The property, now that's where the value lies. Our contract would only ensure that we can negotiate for the best price now, and plan development later. It takes the pressure off you. The real estate developers will leave you alone. You can have some peace and quiet. The law firm will handle any and all proposals for development."

"The law firm, meaning you."

"I would be the executor—act in your behalf."

"And I suppose a valuable prize like my twenty acre patch, as you call it, would stand you in good stead in your firm. Possibly get you that senior partnership you covet."

Edwin blanched, but he did not disagree.

"Ah," Addy sat her cup down and folded her hands in her lap. "Now I understand."

"Time gets away from all of us, Addy. You always call me young, but I'm not young. I'm forty-five years old. You are right. This will mean a senior partnership."

"So," Addy took a deep breath and paused for emphasis, "maybe the names Boll and Sinclair do still mean a little something in this town."

Edwin recoiled slightly. "You're right. I'm sorry. I didn't mean to offend you or the family." He sat back down slowly and paused to compose his words. "The question is, Aunt Addy. The question that is hanging over you, and over me, is what do you want to happen to this place? This property? As far as I know you have no plan, and no plan leaves you and me as your heir to the whim of the market."

Addy's posture relaxed a little. He was right, of course. The truth was she was ignoring the future, ignoring the fact that she was past her ninetieth birthday, and that the world had moved on without her.

Edwin sensed her change in mood and leaned forward in his chair. "Auntie ... "Addy stiffened at the word, but Edwin didn't notice. "I'm not here to take your house or make you move. I just want to help you tie up these loose ends. Let's make a plan."

Addy studied the face across from her. He looks a lot like his mother, she thought. Silly woman. I never could abide her constant social climbing. She folded her napkin and smoothed it on her lap. "Actually, I do have a plan, Edwin. In fact, that was what the young lady was doing here just now. She's an historical preservation architect. I've been thinking of finding a way to preserve the house—possibly as a museum for the city."

All color drained from Edwin's face. His jaw dropped, and he sat back in his chair as if recoiling from a slap. "Who has been talking to you? Who puts these ideas in your head? You can't be serious, Auntie!"

"Nothing is firm, of course." Addy's posture straightened as she sensed the upper hand. "But I'm exploring the possibilities."

Edwin glanced at his watch and stood up abruptly. "I have a meeting downtown." He paused and stared down at her. "I can't believe you undertook this idea without consulting me."

"Edwin," Addy stood and drew herself up to her full height to look him square in the eye. "I'm old but I'm not dotty! I have my full faculties! And as long as I do, I'll think for myself. I appreciate your interest in my affairs, but when I need your advice, you will hear from me."

"You obviously do need my advice, Addy." They stood toe to toe for a moment.

"You have one thing confused, Edwin." Addy's voice was sharp and clear. "You aren't my only heir." She waited to see the uncertainty in his eyes. "There's Gladys. I've told Grayson I want her provided for. Remember that." She took a deep breath as though to

14

steady her nerves, but she did not look away.

Edwin looked as though he might explode at first, as though he were holding back a torrent of words. But instead he blinked again and broke eye contact. "I have to go." He stepped around her and headed for the door. "We'll talk about this again!"

Addy listened as the front door rattled shut behind him, and the car engine started. She took a deep breath and looked up at the portrait staring down from above the mantle.

"Well Albert, now what do I do?"

CHAPTER 3

Robyn ate a quick lunch at a deli in her building and then went up the six floors to her new office. The opulence of the marble-trimmed elevator and hallways still amazed her. Barton & Ramsey was not a firm to be taken lightly. Now if she could just measure up. She said a passing hello to the secretary and then settled into unpacking boxes in her own tiny cubicle. She had emptied several cartons of books and papers and arranged them on her shelves when Dalton Ramsey stuck his head in her door and knocked twice on the frame. "Busy?"

"Hi, come in. I was just trying to get settled a little."

"Looks good." He flashed a grin.

Robyn straightened from her crouched position over the boxes.

"I've just gotten off the phone with Adeline Sinclair. You seem to have made quite an impression on her. How did you find her?"

Robyn answered with a blank look while she tried to identify the name. "I don't believe I've met anyone named Sinclair."

"Little lady, in her nineties. With the big house."

"Oh!" I didn't know her name. She wasn't exactly interested in talking to me, I thought."

"Well, she is now. How did you manage to meet her?"

"Pure accident. I was looking for an apartment"

"Ah."

"She called here? How did she find me?"

"Never underestimate Adeline Sinclair. She was checking you out. Wanted a reference that you are who you say you are."

"So, who did you tell her I am?"

"My brilliant new architect, who needs a roof over her head."

"And did I pass muster?"

"I believe so. She asked me to invite you out for lunch tomorrow. That's probably a good sign."

"You've seen her house, I suppose."

Ramsey smiled and raised his eyebrows. "Only from the road. Adeline doesn't favor many people with tours, I'm afraid."

"She didn't seem at all interested in seeing me this morning, either."

"Well, she's changed her mind."

"So, is there something I need to know about all this before I go charging in?"

"Oh yes, there are a few things." He laughed softly. "Which brings me to my mission. My wife is looking forward to meeting you. She called to invite you to dinner tonight. Do you have plans?"

"No, no, I don't."

"Good, we can cover all this there. Are you ready to

go now?" He glanced around at the clutter.

Robyn pushed at her flattened hair. "I'm afraid I'm sort of a mess."

"You look fine." This is nothing formal. Just the three of us over Diane's famous pot roast. Do you have your car here?"

"Yes"

"Fine, you can follow me now, and I'll show you the way. We don't live far, and we won't keep you out late."

"Thank you, that sounds wonderful."

True to his word, Dalton Ramsey's house was only a short distance, nestled back in a well manicured neighborhood off Turtle Creek Blvd. Georgian architecture, very academic looking, Robyn thought. His wife was lovely. Robyn felt welcome from the first, and as Ramsey had promised, the atmosphere was informal and friendly. She could have been at home in her mother's kitchen. The pot roast was delicious.

"Ramsey tells me you are still in a hotel."

"Yes, I'm looking for a place though. Hopefully close to downtown."

"There are some lovely places not far from here."

"But probably out of my price range, I'm afraid."

"The high rises along Turtle Creek, maybe, but there are others not so pricey I would think."

"Well, I hope so. I'm looking."

"So that's how you found the old house." Ramsey said.

"Yes, I was wandering around and stumbled on to it."

Ramsey glanced at his wife over his glasses. "Robyn met Adeline Sinclair today."

"Really!" Diane turned full attention on Robyn. "I'm very impressed. And how did that come to pass?"

"Bad traffic." Robyn laughed. "I turned down her lane to avoid a traffic jam on Swiss Avenue and wound up asking her if she had a room to rent."

The Ramseys chuckled softly at the wonder of it.

"I had no idea this was such a topic of interest," Robyn said. "You told me you would fill me in."

"Yes, well Adeline Sinclair doesn't welcome visitors that often. She is the last of one of our original Dallas families. Her ancestors carried a lot of weight in this community. She's in her nineties and almost a recluse today. Her house that you stumbled on is one of the oldest standing structures in the city. Lots of history there. We tried years ago to interest her in sharing her family story with us and maybe taking steps to preserve the property, but Adeline resists intrusion. She has dedicated her life to the memory of her father's family, Boll, and the memory of her late husband, Albert Sinclair. He was a war hero in World War II. But she has done all this on her own and ignored our efforts."

"So why do you think she has changed her mind and wants to see me tomorrow?"

"Robyn has a lunch invitation tomorrow."

"Amazing! How ever did you manage that?"

"I have no idea. When I left her today, she dismissed me quite finally. Mr. Ramsey told me about the invitation just before we got here."

"Not so formal, now. Everyone calls me Ramsey."

"Ramsey," Robyn repeated with a smile and a nod.

He continued, "I would not begin to guess about her reasons. But if she suddenly suggests that she wants to take steps to preserve that house, agree and tell her I'll be glad to talk with her."

"And if she just wants to rent me a room?"

"That's up to you, but from my standpoint any chance to get to know that little lady is a positive."

"So, Barton & Ramsey would be interested in her house?"

"Most definitely. Historic preservation is a personal hobby of mine. Your work in renovation was what caught my eye in your resume. New construction pays the rent, of course, but Diane and I are very committed to preserving the past. Like I said when you signed with us, I plan to put you right to work."

"That section of Swiss Avenue is just beginning to draw redevelopment attention," Diane said. "There are several groups that are working to save some of the old landmarks as the land gets bought up."

"You said the house is one of the older structures in the city."

"We believe so. Late 1880s, we think. My guess is that it has been added to several times over the years, but there doesn't seem to be any official record."

"Who was the original owner?"

"Adeline Sinclair's great-grandfather Henry Boll was the original landowner. The Boll family came here in 1856 as part of the La Reunion colony. But her grandfather Jacob Boll actually built the existing house sometime in the 1880s.

"I've never heard of the La Reunion colony."

"It was a Utopian community of Free Thinkers settled by European families, mostly French and Swiss. Some German and Belgian too, I think. It was supposed to be a social experiment. Everything would be jointly owned by the group."

"That's amazing! I had no idea."

"A man by the name of Considerante was the leader, Victor Considerante. He hoped to encourage people to abandon the class distinction of Europe. The people were all well educated and gifted craftsmen. They were a marked departure from most of the frontier stock that settled Dallas."

"Where was the colony?"

"Just across the Trinity River from downtown. But it didn't last long. Most of the settlers were ill-suited for farming in our Texas climate, and of course, the socialism part didn't work."

"Sounds familiar."

"Exactly. It's the same story as today. The people who were willing to work soon got tired of supporting the ones who refused. Anyway, what the colonists did discover was that the village of Dallas was hungry for their skills. They could cross the Trinity River into Dallas and be well paid for their work. Free enterprise won out."

"So the settlers just moved across the river?"

"Yes, some went in other directions, but most came to Dallas. Within three years the colony was gone. There is evidence of the colonists all across the city. Reverchon Park was named for one of the colonists. Julian Reverchon had a farm where Dallas Country Club is today. He raised flowers and vegetables. He became internationally know as a botanist and taught at Baylor Medical School in his later years. Fretz Park is named for another colonist, Emil Fretz, one of the cities first park commissioners."

"Well, Robyn." Diane whispered, "You have him started now. Ramsey loves history. He can go on all night."

"That's wonderful! I love history, also. Especially these types of connections."

"Diane's right. It's one of my favorite pursuits.

The buildings, the street names, why something was built and by whom. There's a lot of street connections. Swiss Avenue, of course, and then Nussbaumer, Boll, Cantegrel, Santerre. Santerre was one of the few real farmers in the colony. His street is out at the old colony site. Remond Street is named for Emil Remond, the first man to manufacture cement from Dallas limestone. And there are several other streets. Henry Boll, Adeline's ancestor, was a butcher by trade, but he bought a farm northeast of town and wound up making a fortune in real estate. The house you found, of course, was built years later, but we think it was at the site of Boll's original farmstead."

"And Adeline hasn't been interested in preserving the family history?"

"Oh, she's interested in the history all right. Just not in our participation. She has mainly put her efforts toward preserving the memories of her parents, Luis and Margarette Boll, and her late husband, Albert Sinclair. You see the names scattered across different projects in the city. There's a Sinclair Memorial Garden at the Arboretum and a Boll Plaza downtown. Adeline Sinclair has been a standout in benevolent projects for more than a half-century. But she's tapered off in the last few years."

"From what I saw, the house and grounds haven't been maintained all that well."

"I doubt that her estate is as large as it once was. A gardener probably isn't in her budget now."

So what we would hope is, Mrs. Sinclair would be agreeable to letting us examine the house and assess its historic value?"

"And let us help her preserve the property in some way. She has twenty acres remaining. The whole area has been overlooked until just recently, but it's on the edge of downtown. It couldn't stay hidden forever."

"It sounds very interesting."

"So, were you doing historic preservation work in Atlanta?" Diane asked.

"No, not in Atlanta. Just out of college I worked with a firm in New York for a year. I helped restore several colonial structures."

"I was telling Diane that you come highly recommended by your Atlanta firm, Starnes & Jacobs, I believe?" Ramsey asked.

Robyn nodded.

"They did the Arts Center in Atlanta, didn't they? Did you work on that?"

"Yes, I did. I was on the team." She smiled. "I can't take much credit for the design, but I put in my hours on the details, I can assure you."

"But Ramsey tells me you have been out of the field for the last two years."

"I had some health issues, but that's all behind me now."

."I'm sorry to hear that," Ramsey said.

We don't want to pry," Diane added quickly

"No, it's quite all right." Robyn stiffened. "I'm sure you have questions. I was in an automobile accident. It has taken two years to recover. But I'm fine now."

"Of course," Diane and Ramsey exchanged quick glances.

There was an awkward pause, until Diane spoke up. "So, have you had a chance to look our city over yet?"

"No, not really." Robyn was grateful for the conversation shift. "I'm looking forward to it though."

"Ramsey and I can be your guides. There's lots of interesting things to see from a tourist stand point, and the shopping is wonderful."

"Certainly," Ramsey said, "but I'll leave the shopping to you two."

The rest of the evening was more small talk. Robyn relaxed and gave herself over to polite conversation.

The hall clock chimed eight.

"Well, that's my cue, I think." Robyn turned to Diane. "Thank you so much for the wonderful dinner.

"My pleasure. Ramsey has been so excited about having you come to work with him. I'm just glad to get to meet you at last. We need to talk some more about things other than shopping and architecture!" She gave Robyn a little wink.

"Yes, we need to do that." Robyn's warning system sounded in the back of her head. There would be more questions. "Let me help you clear the table."

"No, no, I'll take care of all that. You get to be the guest."

"Well, then," Robyn took in a deep breath. "I will just be going."

"You think you can you find your way back to the hotel all right?"

"No problem. I'm learning the streets quickly. I'll see you tomorrow."

Safe in her car, Robyn waved good-bye to the Ramseys, the two of them tall and slender, Ramsey's arm around his wife's shoulders, both of them smiling and waving from their front step. Robyn relaxed into the car seat. She felt as if she had just dodged a bullet. As she drove away she reviewed the conversation.

My girl, she lectured herself, you know there are going to be questions. People will ask questions. Two years is a long time. You can handle this better. She was suddenly as exhausted as though she had been running. Please, now if she could only sleep.

CHAPTER 4

It was always the same dream. There was a doorway in shadow. It would slowly open and there was someone standing there. Sometimes she knew the person, most of the time it was an unfamiliar face, but her part was always the same. She was explaining, or trying to explain why the baby was not there. Over and over she saw the same door, the same scene, gave the same message. Somewhere in her struggle, she would call frantically to Jonathan, call for his help, but the help never came. And in her struggle she would awaken, shaking, bathed in sweat, exhausted and sad, sad past all expression.

Robyn lay perfectly still, feeling the pounding of her heart, gasping for breath. And again, once again, the sadness washed over her. It was not a dream. The baby was gone, and Jonathan was gone. They were gone.

In the first months after she had regained consciousness Robyn had cried tears unending, with pain that seared her insides. But over the last year she had no tears left, just the pain, late at night, and the dream.

Robyn glanced at the clock on the bedside table, 5:15. Ah, she had done better. She had slept for three hours.

She lay back and stared at the blackness above her. Jonathan. She could almost see his face. Why? Why am I still here?

At 6:00 she got up and showered. She dressed and went down to the coffee shop for breakfast. A process, a routine, one step in front of the other. It was the only way. Everyone said so.

She drove to the office on streets that were becoming familiar. One step at a time, she repeated the mantra, one step at a time.

Her cell phone rang as she pulled into the parking garage. Robyn glanced at the number. "Hello, Mother. Good morning!"

"Good morning! I hope I've caught you before you got to work. Is it okay? Can you talk?"

"Yes, I'm still in my car."

"Well, I can't get used to the time change yet. I have to keep reminding myself you are an hour behind us. I try not to call too early. How are you? Did you sleep well?"

Robyn smiled at the question. "Yes, better."

"Have you found an apartment yet?"

"No, but I'm looking. There are some nice places near here."

"Your Aunt Merideth called, and we're going to lunch today. Remember that little tearoom where you used to meet us sometimes? We're going there."

"Well, tell her hello for me."

"Oh, I miss you so much, sweetheart. I wish you could join us."

"I miss you too, Mom. But I just had to make the move."

26

"I know, I know, but I can't help but worry. Are you feeling okay?"

"I'm fine, Mom. You've got to stop worrying so much. I'll be fine." Robyn locked her car. "Look, I'm here now. I've got to run. I'll call as soon as I've found a place to live. You and Dad can come out to see me then. Okay?"

"Yes, we'll do that. Maybe you will have found Shelby by then. Have a wonderful day. I love you."

"Yes, maybe. I love you, too. Good bye."

Robyn snapped the phone shut and slipped it into her bag. She gave a deep sigh of relief. The phone call was out of the way for another day. She was free. At the same instant she felt guilty. Free from what? The love and concern of her parents? Two people who had never been anything but supportive and caring?

But she was doing the right thing, she told herself. She had to break away. Start over, if that was possible. And the last year had proven she could not do that under the watchful eyes of her parents and the network of friends and family clustered around her in Atlanta. Their intentions were good, but she saw the sorrow in their eyes, heard the pity in their voices. No, she had to break away, or the grief would surely kill her.

The elevator door slid open on the sixth floor. Robyn surveyed the room as she stepped out. Her new life, her new world.

The secretary looked up and smiled. "Good morning, Ramsey left a message that he had some information for you. He's in his office now, if you want to go in."

"Thank you, Mira." Robyn dropped her briefcase off in her cubicle and picked up a legal pad for notes.

Right to work, she thought. This is good!

Ramsey looked up from his desk. "Good morning!"

"Good morning. I so enjoyed dinner last night. Please thank Diane again for me."

"Will do. You were quite a hit. Diane made me promise that I would let you take a long lunch with her soon."

"That would be nice." Robyn paused. "So, Mira said you wanted to see me?"

"Yes. I came in this morning and dug up our file on Addy Sinclair's house. Thought you might want to read over it before lunch today."

"Right. What time is that?

"She said 11:30, I believe."

Robyn took the folder Ramsey offered as she sat down across from him.

"There isn't much first-hand info there," Ramsey said. "Just some background from old newspapers. But it might help you."

Robyn glanced at the notes. "What other projects are out there?"

"Well, Penrow has been buying in the area for years as the old owners died off, and I understand Andover-Warren now owns a large tract on the north side of the Sinclair property. There are plans in the works for several office towers, and I'm sure someone is planning another townhouse complex."

Ramsey looked at her over his glasses, and Robyn smiled at his meaning. It had entered her mind also as she drove around in her apartment search that the rows of apartment buildings might not stand the test of time. Their design might be the beginning of urban blight for the future.

"She mentioned Penrow when I was there."

"Development is coming, and that is a good thing. But the area needs some green space. That's our big arguing point. If we can prove there is something unique and historic about the house, and get Adeline Sinclair to agree, we might wind up with a very special development there."

"Sounds ambitious."

"To say the least. But leave all the intrigue and deal-making to me and the planning committee. Your job is to go make friends with Adeline and see what our chances are. If we do nothing, the house gets leveled when she dies, and another tower goes up."

Ramsey's phone rang, and he reached for it. "Look over the notes and have a nice lunch. I'll talk to you this afternoon."

CHAPTER 5

Robyn knocked on the door at promptly 11:30. Again she appraised her reflection in the beveled glass, and this time noted with satisfaction that her hair looked better. She took a deep breath to calm her nervousness and waited.

Like the day before, she heard the approaching steps, but this time a different face appeared. A younger woman, mid seventies maybe, opened the door. "Miss Merrill?"

"Yes, I'm here to … "

"Come in. Mrs. Sinclair is expecting you." The woman stepped back, and Robyn followed her in. "I'm Gladys Thornton, Mrs. Sinclair's housekeeper." No smile.

"Robyn Merrill."

The woman nodded and turned. "Mrs. Sinclair is waiting in the sunroom. Robyn followed her across the spacious entry and was immediately self-conscious of the noise her shoes made on the polished wooden floor. She rolled up on her toes to lighten her step. That and a large Persian rug did the trick to some effect. At the end of the hall they entered a room like something out of a Victorian novel. Robyn quickly glanced at the heavily carved furniture and rich brocade appointments. An ornate grand piano filled the far end of the room. Not too shabby. Very impressive.

Through another doorway they entered a garden room filled with wicker furniture, potted plants and hanging baskets. The back wall of the room was a series of glass panels. Seated at a round table in the filtered sunlight was Adeline Sinclair, smiling warmly.

"Good morning, Miss Merrill." She offered her hand. "Excuse me from not rising. Please, be seated." Robyn sat where Adeline indicated. "What would you like to drink, dear? We have tea and water."

"Tea would be nice." They both looked at Gladys, who nodded and disappeared into the next room.

"Gladys was gone to visit her family yesterday, so I wasn't prepared to invite you in. I'm so glad you could come today."

"Thank you for the invitation."

Gladys returned with the drinks. "Whose birthday was it, Gladys?"

"My youngest grandniece." She looked at Robyn. "It was her third birthday."

"Oh, how wonderful."

"Gladys is famous for her salads and soups. I hope that is satisfactory for you."

"It sounds very good."

"I suppose you can go ahead and start serving, Gladys. I'm sure Miss, or is it Mrs.?" Adeline waited for an answer.

"Ms."

"Ah yes, the modern form. Ms. Merrill is on a schedule and needs to get back to the office, I would assume."

Gladys disappeared again.

"I'm afraid I didn't introduce myself too well yesterday. I'm Adeline Sinclair. I'm sure your bosses at Barton & Ramsey have filled you in."

"Yes, a little. Mr. Ramsey tells me your family has been quite prominent in Dallas for many years."

"We'll get to that. For now I'm more interested in you. Tell me about yourself.

"Well, ... you know my name, Robyn Merrill."

"How do you spell that?"

"Pardon me?"

"How do you spell your name; with an I or a Y?"

"Y"

"Good," Adeline replied flatly as though Robyn had answered the question correctly. "And your last name, Merrill. How do you spell that, one L or two?"

"Two."

Again the woman nodded her approval. "Go on."

"Yes, well," Robyn paused, a little flustered by the questioning. "I'm an architect. I just joined the firm of Barton & Ramsey."

"From Atlanta." Adeline interrupted.

"From Atlanta, I ... "

"Do you have family there? Brothers or sisters? You mentioned your mother yesterday."

"I have one sister, but not in Atlanta. My mother and father are there. They ... "

"What are their names?'

"Their names? Helen and Randell Jefferson."

"Not Merrill?"

"No."

"Jefferson. So you have been married."

"Yes, I was"

"Divorced?"

"No." Robyn stopped.

Adeline sat waiting for an explanation.

"My husband was killed, Mrs. Sinclair."

"Oh." They sat in silence for a few minutes. "Please forgive me," Adeline said softly. "I'm old and accustomed to saying or asking whatever I please. I should have never overpowered you with questions like this."

"No, it's fine. I still find it hard to put into words, but it's the truth, and I must face it."

After a few minutes of awkward silence Adeline spoke in a kinder tone. "It seems we have something in common, Ms. Merrill. My husband was killed when he was very young, also."

Gladys returned with soup and salad. Grateful for the distraction, they waited while she served.

"This looks wonderful, Gladys."

"Thank you. I'll just be in the kitchen if you need anything."

They watched her walk away and then concentrated on the food, which Robyn noted was delicious.

Adeline ate very little. She paused for a drink of tea. "Let's begin again, and you tell me whatever you please. I promise just to listen."

Robyn took a second to consider what to say. She could feel that some barrier had dropped. Adeline's mood was softer, but one thing was certain. The woman across from her was on some sort of mission today. This was not to be idle chatter. She wanted something.

"What would you like me to tell you?"

Adeline pushed at her salad. "Well, I know your name and I know your employer. I suppose I want

33

to know how you found my house, and why you are interested in it." She chose another bite of salad as she waited for answer.

"How I found your house." Robyn paused to organize her thoughts. "Well, that is an interesting story, I suppose. I was apartment hunting yesterday and got caught in some bad traffic on Swiss Avenue. As strange as it sounds, I saw your sign purely by accident and turned down your lane."

Adeline's lips formed a slight smile, but her eyes conveyed wary suspicion. "So your firm didn't send you here?"

"No, they did not. Once I had turned in, I realized I couldn't back out into that traffic, so I came down the lane to turn around. By then I had gotten a good look at the house, and frankly, I was hooked." Robyn laughed softly, but Adeline didn't join in. "I love old houses, you see. I grew up in one much like this, although not this grand, I think." Robyn glanced around at the surrounding room.

"Pardon me for my reservations, Ms. Merrill, but I've been the object of curiosity before." Adeline raised her gaze slightly and inspected her through the lower part of her glasses.

"So why did you invite me today?"

Adeline laughed in surprise at Robyn's directness. "Why indeed, Ms. Merrill." She folded her napkin and placed it on the table. "Would you like a short tour of the house before dessert?"

"That would be nice."

Adeline stood and steadied herself for a second with her hand on her chair. She was tall and slender. Almost as tall as Robyn. Her posture was straight, Robyn noted. Dressed in a mauve silk skirt and blouse with the loveliest pearl necklace Robyn had ever seen,

Adeline was the picture of graceful age and good breeding.

"Let's go to the library first. That is my favorite room." Adeline led the way to a side door of the sun room. "My father had this room added," she called back over her shoulder. "He copied it from libraries he saw in Europe as a young man."

Robyn stepped through the doorway and was captivated by walls of book shelves on all sides. Filtered light streamed in from the end of the room where ten-foot stained-glass windows filled an alcove. The center of the room held seating areas of over-stuffed chairs and sofas. On one wall was a large fireplace. It could be the reading room of a small college. "This is wonderful!"

Adeline watched Robyn's reaction and smiled. "It's lovely, isn't it? I've tried to maintain it as my father intended."

Robyn stared awestruck at the detail in the room. "When was this added?"

"My father, Luis Boll, had this built in 1924." She waited patiently for Robyn to finish her survey. "I was married in this room," she added.

"The books are wonderful. Quite a collection."

"Credit my father and mother. They loved books. There are quite a few rare editions here, I'm told. I had it cataloged and organized a few years back." She gestured toward the end of the room and Robyn followed her lead.

Adeline opened a side door to her left leading into the room with the grand piano. "You saw this music room as you came in." She stood to one side so Robyn could look.

"Yes, that's a wonderful piano. Do you play?'

"Poorly, I'm afraid." Adeline laughed. "My parents spent a fortune on my lessons, but I'm afraid I disappointed them. I love to hear it played though. My grandparents and parents were famous for their concerts here. Several well known artists entertained guests here over the years. The acoustics in the room are wonderful. Something to do with the stone walls."

Robyn followed her gaze and noted for the first time that the walls of the entire room were, in fact, limestone. She looked back into the library to compare. The walls there were covered by a rich brocade pattern paper.

Adeline called her attention back to the tour. "Back this way is the main parlor."

Robyn followed, making mental notes about the structure as she walked.

The parlor was everything the name implied. Richly furnished; clusters of photographs on every table, filtered light from ten-foot windows draped in gorgeous fabric. Adeline pushed aside a curtain and unlatched a door. She swung the doors back to let in more light and air. Robyn looked around the room and realized there were no windows. All the openings were French doors leading out to the veranda.

She laughed softly in delight. "That is wonderful. I love the doors!"

"Yes, a bit unusual for Texas, I suppose." Adeline seemed pleased with her reaction. She opened another door. "My grandparents' touch. They wanted a European influence in the house."

Gladys appeared with a tray of desserts. They settled on a velvet sofa before the fireplace and finished their lunch.

"So you see, Ms. Merrill: I'm rather fond of my house." Adeline said after a time.

"Yes, and I can see why. It is lovely, and I'm sure the history tells a wonderful story."

36

"The house has changed over the years. Each generation has added to it in some way. Not so much with me. I renovated the plumbing and the kitchen sometime back, added central air. And, of course, I added the elevator there in the front hall. I'm afraid these old bones don't like the stairs anymore."

"I would say those were wise choices."

"If my husband had lived ... " She glanced up at the portrait over the fireplace. "I'm sure we might have made more changes, but not me alone."

I understand your husband was killed in World War II."

"Yes, 1944. He was killed in France they tell me, not long after the invasion."

Robyn looked toward the photograph on the sofa table where Adeline indicated. The same slender man in uniform gazed back at her. Several framed medals sat next to the picture.

"You said your husband was killed. How did he die?'

"Car accident," Robyn looked back at Adeline. "A drunk driver hit the car head-on. Nothing as glorious as battle, I'm afraid."

"I'm sorry, dear. I'm sorry we share that experience." They sat in awkward silence for a few moments before Robyn spoke.

"Your house is lovely, Mrs. Sinclair."

"Call me Adeline or Addy. Whichever you choose. Everyone does. And I'll call you Robyn. Is that acceptable?"

"Yes, very much so."

"I hope we can be friends." Adeline continued. "That's one of the saddest parts of long life, you know. Your friends die off. I have very few left, I'm afraid. So you will be my new young friend." She patted

Robyn's hand. "Now tell me why you are interested in my house. You asked me why I invited you. I'll return the question. Why did you come?"

Robyn smiled. "Yes, well, as I said before, I turned up at your doorstep yesterday because of your sign. The 'Room for Rent' sign."

"One of my crazy ideas a few years back. There was a room above the garage at that time. A remodeled barn actually, and a friend of mine convinced me I might rent it out in exchange for a driver and yard man. My yard man had gotten too old, and I was tired of fighting traffic. But it didn't work out. I made other arrangements with a service and forgot about the sign."

"So there is no room?"

"No, the building was unsound. I had it torn down several years ago. There's nothing left but the foundation. It wouldn't have been suitable for you anyway. Not for a young woman alone."

"I see. Well, that takes care of my reason for being here. Now it's your turn. Why did you invite me today?" Robyn wasn't about to be the first one to broach the topic of preserving the house."

"I felt badly about turning you away so abruptly yesterday. I get few visitors these days." Adeline paused as though she was planning her next words. "And I was intrigued by your confession of loving old houses. You don't find that often in the young, you know."

"As I said earlier, I grew up in a smaller version of this house in Atlanta. I've always loved the style. My mother inherited our house. The men in her family were important railroad people after the Civil War— new money in the South back then." Robyn smiled. "My father's family was Old South. They 'lost everything in the War,' as they say in Atlanta, and they have never quite recovered. But he married well."

"My father was in railroads." Adeline said. "His father before him was a doctor. My great-grandfather, Henry Boll, made his fortune in real estate. This house was built and remodeled several times by the generations. It was the center of the social scene in Dallas for many years. I've tried to maintain it, to honor the memories of my people, but I'm not that active today." She gestured toward the portrait again. "My husband, Albert Sinclair, was a railroad man like my father. I suppose people would say he married well, also. Albert had no family, but he was very smart, very ambitious. My father took him under his wing since he had no sons. I was an only child." Adeline motioned toward a photograph of a small boy gazing solemnly from a gilded frame on the mantle. "My brother died of influenza in 1914, before I was born. You mentioned a sister earlier. Are you close?"

"No."

Adeline glanced back at Robyn, responding to the shortness in her answer.

"I haven't talked to her is several years. Her choice. But that may change soon. She lives here in Dallas, I understand. I mean to look her up."

"Family is important." Adeline glanced again at the photographs. "I realize that very clearly now that it is almost gone. If Albert had survived the war, we might have had quite a different life, children. But me alone …"

"And you never considered marrying again?"

"No," Adeline shook her head ever so slightly as though slightly scandalized by the question, "No."

"I see."

"So now I'm in the twilight of my years as they say. I'm ninety years old. That surprises me sometimes when I think about it. But I know I probably don't have many years left. I need to make plans for my house." Adeline looked around as she spoke. So, I thought maybe it was fate that brought you here yesterday."

"I take it you have been approached about your house before? You mentioned Penrow Corporation yesterday."

"I'm afraid Penrow, and everyone else for that matter, is interested in my land, not my house."

"I'm sure the land is very valuable."

"Yes, so I've been told." Adeline looked out at the view across the lawn. "I have a great nephew once removed, my late cousin's grandson and closest relative. You saw him yesterday, I believe, as you were leaving."

The guard dog, Robyn thought, remembering her unfriendly encounter.

"Edwin Bennett. He's a lawyer here in the city and very ambitions to control my house. We were close when he was a boy. Sort of the child or grandchild I never had." A whisper of a smile crossed her lips. "I'm afraid we've grown apart over the years. He's not a bad sort, I suppose, just rather inept and little eager to step into my shoes. I..., I told a little white lie yesterday, I'm embarrassed to admit. I told him that you and I had been discussing preserving my house." Adeline watched for Robyn's reaction to her confession. "I'm covering my tracks today, Robyn. Locking the barn door after the horse is loose, as they say."

"I see."

"But when I realized you were truly interested in my house, I thought ... "

"My boss, Mr. Ramsey, hired me, he said, because he and his wife are very dedicated to historical preservation. I worked in the field a few years back. He very much wants to talk to you about your house."

"If he is truly interested in the house as you say and not just the land, I would be willing to talk to him. Could you arrange that for me?"

"Yes I can."

They both stood up slowly. "I'll talk to Mr. Ramsey this afternoon. I'm sure he and his wife will be very excited to know there is a chance to preserve this lovely place."

"Let's keep this private for now." Adeline cautioned. "I need to know what plans your Mr. Ramsey has before I agree to any action. No reason to upset Edwin just yet."

"I understand. Now can I help you close the parlor before I go?"

"That is very thoughtful." They each took separate doors and Adeline waited for Robyn by the last one. "You can go out here, if you wish."

They stepped through the opening onto the front veranda next to the rocking chairs. Robyn walked to the railing to survey the lawn, and Adeline joined her. Here and there was evidence of landscaped beds, long uncared for, but still attractive in a graceful, unkept way.

"It's a glorious day today." Adeline turned her face up to the sun. "Most days are, you know, but we just don't always acknowledge it."

"This place is absolutely beautiful, Adeline. I had no idea I was stumbling on to such a treasure yesterday."

"Thank you. It is such a relief to me to see that you appreciate it. For the first time in a long time, I'm very excited about the future. You are an interesting young woman, Robyn. I like your direct manner. I think we can work together."

Robyn extended her hand, and Adeline grasped it

in both of hers. "And, I do believe we were meant to meet, Robyn. Life makes its own way in matters like this."

"I think you may be right, Adeline."

CHAPTER 6

"That's great! Good work!" Ramsey said when Robyn reported on her meeting with Adeline Sinclair. "We need to do some brainstorming on this. Get organized before we meet with her. What was your impression of the house over all?"

Good condition considering its age. Some very interesting design points. I've got some questions jotted down."

"Get started on any old records you can find. City hall has done a good job of preserving what they have, but their records are spotty. There weren't many requirements or permits in the 1800s. Call Mrs. Sinclair and set a get-acquainted meeting next week. Then pull together whatever you can find. Bring your questions, and the two of us can go over them. Better yet, let me talk to Diane. She has done this several times on other houses with the Heritage League. The three of us should talk." Ramsey was writing furiously as he spoke. "By the way, how did the rented room work out?"

"Not good."

"I was talking to Mira this morning. She has a suggestion. It seems the company owns a property on Blackburn that might be perfect. Get the address from her and go take a look. It's pretty upscale, but we can get you a major break on the rent. In the current market, it turns out we have a few vacancies there."

"Thank you, I'll do that."

"Go take a look now. The sooner you can get settled, the sooner we can move on this project."

Like every other city in the United States, Dallas was experiencing a rebirth of downtown living. The flight to the suburbs of the last fifty years had bled the hearts out of urban areas all over the country, and the explosion of shopping malls had sealed the deal. With the exception of maybe New York and Chicago, most cities had slowly drifted outward, and Dallas was no different. Gone were the downtown theaters shoulder to shoulder on Elm Street and the row on row of shops snuggled up to Neiman Marcus or Sanger Harris. Even the hotels had moved out to crossways of freeways and service roads along turnpikes aimed at DFW Airport. Robyn knew the model well. Sprawling neighborhoods with green belts, cavernous shopping malls, and acres of parking.

But with the new century, the tide had turned. Clusters of high rises had sprung up. Multi-use instant neighborhoods close to downtown were making their mark.

The building on Blackburn was one of the new

design. Close in so that the young "30-somethings" could forgo the hour commute and walk to work. And their favorite bistro or coffee shop was a few flights down at street level. Robyn liked the concept. It gave a feeling of small town closeness to a city environment. The apartments weren't cheap though. Way out of the price range of an entry level architect as a rule. But then, that was the advantage of working for a firm that owned the building, she reasoned. She parked on the street and went to look the place over.

The apartment was perfect. Four floors up. High enough above the street to avoid the noise, low enough for fire truck ladders. Okay, so she was a worrier, but, still, too high bothered her. Close to the office. She could walk to work and get some exercise, she reasoned, and the first floor of the building consisted of shops and restaurants. She signed the lease and took the keys. It was good to get that settled. Quick trip to a furniture store, order her stuff from storage, and she could be moved by Sunday.

⚬⚬⚬⚬⚬⚬

The rest of the week Robyn spent buried in the archives at City Hall and the Old County Courthouse. She turned up little, except tax records and plats of the town lots. County records were the same. Adeline's ancestors did pop up often in the early boards and councils of the town, but not dealing with the house. Unless Adeline had the original plans in her attic, they would have to analyze and identify the materials on site and try to trace them back.

First step would be to get Adeline's permission to examine the house. Robyn wrote up her notes. No, she corrected herself. First step was the meeting with the Ramseys. It was set for Monday morning.

On Saturday, Diane took her on a whirlwind tour of the underbelly of the Trade Mart district. Wonderful things! Overstuffed warehouses with everything an apartment could possibly need and at bargain prices. By Saturday evening she had a bed to sleep in, a sofa to 'veg' on, and a table for piling her stuff. Her boxes from storage were stacked against the wall. The place looked like a college dorm room, but it was a start. She could take her time unpacking. She had brought little with her; as little as possible, hoping to leave her old life behind.

When she awoke at 3:00 A.M. that morning, she opened the box that weighed heaviest on her mind. Her photos, packed carefully in a jumble of shredded paper, had made the trip unscathed. She lined them up on the table. Her parents, she and her sister at ages nine and six, mugging for the camera in their Halloween costumes. As she remembered it, Shelby had been in one of her furious pouts that night because her costume was homemade and not store-bought. Her framed diploma from Georgia Tech, her grandparents at their fiftieth wedding anniversary party, the house off Peachtree Street.

She lifted the frame out carefully. Jonathon. An enlargement of a snapshot she had taken on their honeymoon. They were back-packing in Yosemite. He had looked up when she called his name, and she had caught him unaware, all his shyness about cameras not in evidence. Just that wonderful smile and look of pleasure at hearing her say his name. And she was crying, sobbing as though the pain was new.

What was she doing here? How could this happen? Her life had been so planned. She was so happy as Mrs. Jonathon Merrill. Jonathon. The baby. She had gladly placed her career on hold when she found out she was pregnant. They bought a bigger house. She was all set to be the mom. The play date mom, the PTA mom, the soccer mom.

They decorated the nursery and stocked it with tiny little clothes and a confusing array of gadgets everyone swore a baby needed. They made name lists and debated whether to find out the sex or be surprised. The future looked so clear, just reach out and gather it in.

But it was gone in a grinding flash. All gone. Jonathon and the baby. And she was robbed even of the funeral. When she regained consciousness four months later, it was as if he and the baby were only a dream. Gone. Torn away by the roots leaving her alone. Who was she now? Who would she ever be?

As the sun rose, light slid in her balcony door and eased across to her. She had cried herself out somewhere before dawn. Now she sat drained of energy and watched morning come.

So here she was. Alone, a thousand miles from all the people who had made her unable to forget. But what now? Was the pain any less? Did she feel any different?

Would she ever be able to feel anything but lost again? She glanced around at the room, at the boxes and scattered paper. Yet here she was.

Buck up girl, she told herself. This was your bright idea. Get up, get moving, keep swimming. She dressed in her comfy sweats and went downstairs to check out the new neighborhood. The people flowed around her, bits of conversation brushing against her, laughter, smiles. She found a table on the coffee shop sidewalk. It was a lost day spent behind dark glasses over ridiculously expensive cups of coffee, but she made it. Alone in a crowd, she watched life in the shops ebb and flow around her. No one to explain to, no one she knew. Yes, Dallas was a good idea. She would keep trying.

CHAPTER 7

Dalton Ramsey proved to be the master of charm when Robyn introduced him to Adeline. After only a half hour of polite exchange, Robyn could sense that they were going to be able to work together. The three of them were sitting in the parlor under Albert Sinclair's portrait.

"I know it's an old house, but I think it still has something to offer even after all these years." Adeline said.

"I think so too, Mrs. Sinclair."

"Please call me Adeline or Addy. Everyone does."

"And I'm Ramsey to all my friends, Adeline."

Addy took a deep breath. "Well, Ramsey, how do we begin?"

"First we need to establish that the house is of historic interest. If we can do that we can get historic designation. and it will be protected. We want city, county, state, perhaps even national recognition if we can document. Do you have any records on the construction of the house? Drawings, building receipts, journals?"

"Very little that I can recall at this moment, but there might be records somewhere."

"I don't think city records are going to tell us much." Ramsey glanced at Robyn for backup.

"This area wasn't incorporated into Dallas until some years after this house was built," Robyn interjected. "County records would be our source."

"Yes, I'm sure that is true. This was farm land when my great-grandfather first settled here."

"Do you still have the location of his homestead within these twenty acres? Ramsey asked.

"Adeline smiled. "I would say so. My grandparents built their home on the same site as the original house."

"Really." Ramsey glanced around the room. "Do you have records on the original house, you think?"

"Very little in writing, I'm afraid."

"Did the builders in 1889 use materials from the first house in the second construction?"

Adeline smiled. "I think there is a misunderstanding here." She rose slowly taking time to secure her balance. "I think it's time for a tour."

Ramsey and Robyn exchanged glances and rose to follow her. At the front hall, Adeline paused and swept her hand out in a presenting motion. "All this, the dining room, the entry, the parlor. All this is my grandparents' construction from the 1880s.

This," She stretched out her hand toward the back wall of the entry. "Is the original house."

Ramsey and Robyn followed her motion and then stared in confusion. After a moment Ramsey recovered his voice. "The original house?

"My grandparents built their house around the original. It's the core of the house."

"The farm house?"

Adeline nodded and led the way back to the music room.

Ramsey placed his hand on the limestone wall and glanced back toward the entry. "The original house," he said again. "This is amazing!" He laughed and patted the wall. The original house from 18 what?"

"1858, I believe, is when my great-grandparents began building."

"Adeline, you definitely have a treasure here. I guarantee, Barton & Ramsey will see to it that this house is never destroyed."

"I want something note-worthy to come out of this, Ramsey." Adeline cautioned. "Keep that in mind. Just saving the house isn't enough. I don't want it to wind up squeezed in between apartment buildings."

"No, I assure you, we will find a plan that suits your desires. We'll get right on the project."

Robyn lagged behind and watched as Adeline showed Ramsey the music room and the library and back to the parlor. Now that she understood the role of the old farmhouse, she looked for construction clues as she walked. They crossed the entry again to the dining room.

"My grandfather had this table built for the room. He and my grandmother had six children. When the children left home to start their own families, they took their chairs with them. My father was the youngest son. He and my mother lived here to care for his parents and inherited the house when they died. My father's and my grandparents' chairs are still here." She motioned to the head of the table. The three ornately carved chair backs stood in contrast to the rest.

"They're beautiful." Robyn ran her hand over the design.

"Carved by one of the artisans from the old La Reunion Colony." Adeline said. She turned to look at Ramsey "You know the colony connection, I suppose."

Yes, I was filling Robyn in last week." Ramsey said.

"I'd never heard of the colony before. That is a wonderful story."

"Yes, there should be many other connections in the construction."

"So," Robyn said. "We have our work cut out for us, I would say."

Adeline smiled and clasped her hands in satisfaction. "Wonderful!"

"We'll go back to the office and put our heads together. As soon as we have a plan of action I'll call you. We should have some rough ideas in the next few weeks. Will that be satisfactory?" Ramsey asked.

"I look forward to it."

"Meanwhile, do you have any records here that might help us? It would be good if our researchers could get a look at them."

"I would prefer it if Robyn did that." She turned to Robyn. "You can bring help, but I don't want strangers here unescorted. There are files from my father in his study upstairs. I have no idea what you will find, but you are welcome to them." Adeline patted Robyn's arm. "At my age the family secrets don't carry much weight, I suppose."

"Your secrets are safe with me, Adeline."

"Come prepared for dusty work. You can start anytime. I'll tell Gladys you are coming."

"I'll clear everything with the office and start ..." She glanced at Ramsey. "Next week?" He nodded in agreement.

They left by the front door this time.

"I would say that went well," Ramsey offered when they were in the car. "Good work."

"Now the fun begins."

"I can't wait to tell Diane about this. She isn't going to believe it."

Addy stayed at the door until their car backed around and headed down the drive.

So it would come true, her dream of having this place survive after she was gone. Of course, there could still be problems. She knew that, but now, after meeting these young people, she felt hopeful. And Edwin..., well, she would still have to contend with Edwin, but it could be worked out. She took a long satisfying deep breath and went to tell Gladys.

The phone in the front hall rang just as she stepped into the kitchen. Adeline hesitated before she turned back to answer it. Such a bother.

"Hello?"

"Adeline, oh, it's you!" It was Harriet Campbell. Adeline settled herself in the chair by the phone. Harriet's calls always lasted a while.

"Yes, it's me." Addy answered with a slight laugh in her voice. Harriet was a dear old friend, but always a little rattled, it seemed. "Of course, it's me. How are you, dear?"

"Well, I was just so frightened! I told myself it was just a mistake, but still it was such a shock seeing your name like that."

"My name? What are you talking about, dear. Slow down and explain."

"I'm in Houston at my granddaughter's house. Molly brought me down for a visit. Did I tell you about that?"

"Yes, you did. Are you having a good time?"

"Yes, wonderful, or at least it was wonderful. I was so upset I just had to call. I had to hear your voice. When I saw your name in the paper, I ... I just didn't know what to think."

"Saw my name? In what paper?"

"The Houston Post. I was just reading. It isn't the same as The Dallas Morning News, but I was making do, and then there you were. At least I thought it was you. It's not a common name, you know, so ..."

"My name in The Houston Post? Whatever for?"

"It scared me so, I just had to call and make sure you were there."

"Harriet, you must calm down. I'm here. Now tell me why I'm in the Houston paper."

"In the obituaries, Addy. Your name is in the obituaries! I was so frightened when I saw it. Mrs. Albert Sinclair, plain as day! ... Addy, are you still there?"

Adeline recovered her voice. "Yes, Harriet, I'm here. You're quite right. That is strange. I'm sure it gave you a start, but I'm fine. I'm here."

"I'm so relieved. But it was strange. It says you, or rather it says this person is ninety-six. You aren't ninety-six, are you?"

"No." Addy laughed. "Don't make it more than it is. You know I'm only ninety, just like you."

"Yes, yes, of course, I know, but ..."

"It's just a coincidence, dear. Don't worry yourself."

"But it goes on to tell more, Addy. It says her husband was a railroad man and was in the war. And it says he was a Mason. Albert was a Mason, wasn't he?

That is just very strange."

"My, I see what you mean. No wonder you were concerned, but I'm fine. Gladys is taking good care of me. When are you coming home, dear?"

"By the weekend, I think. Molly has to be back at work next week. We'll be home soon."

"Well, call me when you get back."

"Yes, yes I will."

Addy heard the phone line go dead as she slowly replaced the receiver. Another Albert Sinclair? A buzz of shock hovered around her. Old worries, long buried.

Nonsense. She shook her head as if to clear it and went to find Gladys. She had the house to think about.

"Is this going to keep Edwin from bothering you, or will you just be inviting more trouble?" Gladys was standing at the sink washing the cups from Addy's visitors.

Addy grimaced slightly. Trust Gladys to cut right to the heart of something. She was voicing the same fear that tugged at her thoughts. "The fact is, Gladys, you may be right, but I have to do something. We have to find someone to take our side. Penrow and Edwin and all the rest won't give up on this."

Gladys nodded. "I just don't want you hurt, or bothered, Addy. I ..."

"Thank you for that, Gladys. You are a dear friend to me. My most trusted friend."

"We've been together a long time."

"And we'll see this through together." Addy reached out a hand to touch the tile countertop. "I just don't want this house to be lost."

"No, not this place." Gladys dried the last cup and wiped her hands on the towel. "I'll see to it that that young lady can get at the papers upstairs. Did I hear the phone just now?"

"Yes, it was Harriet."

"Didn't she go to her granddaughter's for the week?"

"She's in Houston now."

"Is anything wrong?"

"No, she was just checking on me. She saw someone with my name in The Houston Post."

"Your name?"

"You know Harriet. She was all in a dither. It was just a coincidence."

"What did she say?"

Addy laughed softly. "It was in the obituaries. You know how Harriet always has to read them. She called to make sure I was still here."

"Well, I never!

"Yes, I was a little taken back." Addy laughed along with Gladys. Well, I think I'll go look through a few old albums for pictures of the house that might be of help to Robyn."

"You do that. I'll call you when I have lunch on the table."

CHAPTER 8

It took longer than Robyn expected to get started on the house research. There were legal forms to sign and pages of clarification statements to wade through, insurance on Robyn and any other company employee while they worked at the house, detailed descriptions of their purpose in regards to the property. Papers got shuffled between Barton & Ramsey and Adeline. Ramsey's staff took care of most of it, but Addy and Robyn began to make little jokes about all the papers they were signing.

Robyn busied herself studying examples of blue-prints and sketches of houses from the 1850 to 1900 time frame, familiarizing herself with some of the building practices that might be unique to Dallas at that time. Like the houses she knew from the Southeast, the walls in the early homes were not insulated since winters were so mild, but almost every structure included a porch or veranda that provided shade for the long hot summers. In the houses of the 1800s, the windows ran from ceiling to floor and could be opened from both the bottom and the top to provide cross drafts. Of course in Adeline's case, her home had, in place of windows, large French doors that could be opened on both sides of the house to allow breezes to flow through. Robyn also noted the spacing of studs in the walls and the use of batting or narrow strips of wood to form the inside walls of houses. The batting was then covered with cloth and paper. Of course there was one difference at the Boll Mansion. The central room of the house was solid limestone, two feet thick. The original old farm house appeared to be a French design, and the mixture of styles was going to make for interesting work from an architect's stand- point.

One characteristic that stood out was the lack of basements in the homes. Even in the larger homes such as Adeline's, the houses were built on a pier and beam structure, raised above the ground by two or three feet. Buildings sat on foundations of stone, wood, or brick with open space below the flooring. The reason given was the alluvial soil that caused the ground to shift under buildings, and the clay in the soil that tended to swell or shrink according to the ground moisture. Builders in Texas and the southeast constructed their buildings to float on the surface of the land. The job of preserving the old house promised to be interesting.

Diane Ramsey came to the office, and she and Robyn compared ideas and goals for the house and grounds. Diane had some good insight since she had helped write proposals for historic designation for several houses through various volunteer organizations. It was a chance to work together in a relaxed atmosphere. They took a long lunch and just got acquainted.

"Are you settling in here?"

"Absolutely. It's been very welcoming. The apartment is starting to shape up. Thanks again for your help with the furniture."

"It was fun," Diane said.

"You will have to come over to see it once I get the boxes out of there."

"You mentioned wanting some throw pillow that day. I saw some at Preston Center last week that I think would perfectly match your sofa. I almost bought them, but thought I'd check with you first."

"Is it far? Maybe we could run by there today. I haven't had a minute to shop since you and I went."

It was a comfortable association, the kind that slips into true friendship almost immediately. There was the age difference, of course, but Robyn had always felt more comfortable with older people than with her own age group. Diane could be her mother, she supposed, but then her mother was her friend, also.

Eventually the conversation drifted to a more personal level; the fact that Ramsey and Diane had no children. They had married late, Diane explained. They were in their early thirties when they met and near the forty mark when they married. It was a second marriage for both of them. Diane had her own clothing design career at the time, and Ramsey was busy launching his architecture partnership. Then Robyn felt comfortable enough to say she had been married, and the story of the accident came out.

"I'm so sorry. You mentioned the accident, but I didn't know about your husband. How long were you married?"

"Three years. We met in college and married a year after graduation." Robyn felt as though she were sitting to one side listening to herself. It was the first time she had ever told the story. Everyone in Atlanta had just known.

"And you were unconscious for some time, you say? How terrible."

"Severe trauma, they called it. I was pretty badly injured. It took quite a while to heal, and they kept me heavily sedated ... I was pregnant at the time of the accident," she heard herself saying.

Diane's face froze in an expression of surprise and pain. "No ..." The word was only a whisper.

"The baby didn't survive ..." Robyn's eyes shimmered with tears. "That's the first time I've ever said that out loud."

"I'm so sorry."

And the rest of the story spilled out. The flood of sympathy in Atlanta, the good intentions of old friends and family. "I could see I wasn't going to survive there. Two years of that, and I had to make some sort of break. So here I am" She smiled and reached to brush away a tear.

"Has it been better here?"

"Yes, it has." Robyn took a deep breath to help her get control. "New challenges, new people, not so many memories around every corner." They sat in silence for several minutes.

"So." Diane straightened. "We'll file this away in our friendship box, and you never have to mention it again, unless you choose to."

"Thank you for understanding."

They finished lunch in silence, listening to the flow of conversation around them. Robyn felt as if a weight had lifted from her heart. Another step taken. A friend made.

Diane glanced at her watch. "It's only 12:45. Let's run over and look at those throw pillows."

Harriet Campbell called on Wednesday. "I've been back since last week, but I just didn't call. That's a long drive from Houston. I was just exhausted."

"Well, did you have a good time?" Addy asked.

"Yes, it was grand to see everyone. But they are so busy! Running the children to this and that. It was tiring to watch them."

"How old are the little ones now?"

"Seven and four. Gracious, it doesn't seem possible that my granddaughter could have children that old, but she does."

They laughed together. "Time does get away, doesn't it?" Adeline said.

"Did you find out any more about that woman in the paper?" Harriet asked.

"No, no, I haven't. I don't know that I will. It's just a coincidence that we had the same name, I'm sure."

"Yes, but the name and then the rest. It just gave me a start."

"I'm glad you called me so that you wouldn't worry. You need to come over for a visit soon."

"Well, you know since I don't drive anymore, it's hard. Maybe Molly can bring me over one day. Do you still have symphony tickets?"

"Yes, you need to come with us next time Gladys and I go. We could pick you up."

"Let me know the next time you are going, and maybe I can. What else are you up to? Are you feeling well?"

"Feeling wonderful. I've been talking to people about the house. Maybe preserving it in some way."

"It's a lovely old place, but you need to move,

Addy. It's too big for just you and Gladys."

"Well, maybe, but ..."

"I know, but what would you do with your things. I was the same way." Harriet laughed. "But I'm glad I sold. This place I'm at now is very pleasant, and there's always something to do. I play cards twice a week, and mahjong on Wednesday afternoon."

Adeline had heard it all before. She listened in silence.

"Course, my place didn't have the history your house does. I know you want to protect it."

"Maybe I've found a way to do that."

"Really! That's wonderful. You need to get Gladys to bring you over. We're having a luncheon and a speaker next week. Something about writing your memoirs, I think. We could get in a good visit, and you can tell me about your house."

"I might just do that."

"I've got to go to my exercise class. They are motioning to me."

"Yes, well, thanks for calling."

"Addy."

"Yes?"

"I just remembered. About that woman in Houston. The paper also said her husband died at Normandy. He was a decorated hero. Just like your Albert, Addy. Isn't that strange?"

"Yes ... , yes it is, Harriet. Most unusual. You're right about that. Well, good talking to you. I'll be in touch. Goodbye, dear."

Adeline slowly replaced the receiver. Normandy? So many similar things. But still.

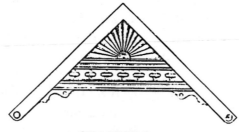

CHAPTER 9

Addy answered the door herself. She thought it best. There was "no love lost" as they say, between Gladys and her great nephew. No sense in stirring in more trouble. Addy knew Gladys was hovering near the hall door, however. There was no use in trying to discourage her.

"Don't you let him bully you now, Addy." Gladys had warned when she learned that Edwin was coming. "Don't you ..."

"I'll call you if I need you, dear. I promise."

As usual Edwin was holding the screen open when she opened the door.

"Morning, Aunt Addy." Edwin entered with a quick look around.

"Let's go to the parlor. Gladys has coffee set up for us." Addy led the way. "I'm glad you could come on such short notice."

Edwin glanced at his watch. "Well, I know we need

to talk. I have a meeting at 11:00, but it's only 10:00 now." He settled himself in a chair. "What's on your mind?"

"We didn't part in the best of ways on your last visit …"

"Yes, well, I'm glad you are thinking more clearly, Auntie. I was just a little taken back by your manner."

"I just thought we needed to talk today. I think there have been some developments in the last few weeks that …"

"Yes, there have been. Interesting you should mention it." Edwin shifted in his chair. "My firm has been contacted by another buyer, Auntie. Now the best thing, I think, would be …"

"Edwin, I mean I have had some developments, not your law firm."

Edwin stopped in mid sentence, and his hand was still raised to make his point. "What do you mean?"

"As I told you in our last talk, I'm pursuing historical designation for the house. The architecture firm of Barton & Ramsey is handling …"

"Historical designation!" Edwin's voice rose to drown her out. "Addy, this is nonsense! This old place couldn't pass any kind of code inspection! The cost of restoring it … Why won't you listen?" He leaned toward her from his chair. "Who is putting these ideas in your head?"

Adeline set her cup down slowly and fixed Edwin with a steady gaze. "Edwin, you need to calm down. I'm trying …"

"Calm down! You call me over here to tell me some fool plan you have to throw this property away, just give it away, and you expect me to sit here and .. ."

"I'm trying to tell you what has transpired so that you can be part of the process and …"

"Part of the process!" Edwin wadded his napkin and tossed it on the coffee table as he rose. "I'll tell you what part I'll take. Barton & Ramsey, you say? I'll take legal action. That's what I'll do. You obviously have lost control here. I'll not stand by and let these people rob you blind."

"Edwin ..." Addy caught sight of Gladys standing in the parlor door with her gaze fixed on Edwin. He looked up and saw her also and glared back.

"I think I've heard enough here. There's nothing left to say for now."

He stormed past Gladys, who turned and followed him to the door.

"Did you put her up to this? Just what do you think you're going to get out of it, Missy?" He grabbed the front doorknob and jerked the door open.

"Satisfaction." Gladys shot back as she swung the door shut in his face.

Addy came out from the parlor, and the two women stared at the closed front door as they listened to Edwin stomp to his car, rev the engine and roar away in a sputter of gravel.

"Well," Addy said as the sound died away. "I suppose I've done it now."

Gladys started to laugh softly. She came back to Addy and put her arm around her shoulders. "You certainly know how to start a fight, dear. I'll give you that."

"I think I'd better call Grayson."

"You do that. Mr. Chandler will know just what to do about that pompous windbag."

Addy sat down by the phone and dialed the number. Grayson Chandler had been her lawyer for thirty years, ever since his father retired and turned his clients over to him. It had rankled Edwin when she wouldn't let him handle her affairs after he finished law school, but there had been no question for Adeline. Grayson had her best interest at heart. She was confident of that.

His secretary forwarded the call to him. "Adeline, how are you today?"

"Hello, Grayson. Something new has surfaced on the house."

"Really. What's the general topic?"

"It's Edwin. I think he plans to make trouble."

Grayson was well aware of the tension between Addy and her great nephew. "Sounds like I need to come by and let you explain it all to me."

"Yes, that would probably be best."

"Let me put you on hold for a second, and I'll check my calendar."

The phone went silent. Thank heavens Grayson didn't have that terrible music on his line like the doctor offices.

Grayson clicked back on. "All right, my secretary tells me I'm free from 9:00 to 10:30 tomorrow. Will that work for you?"

"Wonderful, I'll see you then."

Adeline took a deep breath of satisfaction after she hung up the phone. Grayson would know just what to do. She went to search through more albums. There were some good pictures of the house somewhere, she just knew.

⚬⚬⟨X⟨⟩X⟩⟨⟩⚬⚬

Edwin Bennett was reeling as he rushed down Main toward his office. He couldn't believe this was happening. Addy had no idea the trouble she was causing. No idea! He didn't know how he was going to tell the major partners at the office. The men were going to blow up over this. He wiped sweat from his upper lip.

This was not fair. Not fair. He was doing a good job for the firm. A good job. But it was always just there; the question and the threat. Have you signed your Great Aunt yet? Do we have the contract? Since day one Weldon Shanks had let him know his future at the firm was tied to Adeline Sinclair's property. And he held it over him like a club. Now what could he do? He couldn't force her to sign over the property. But Shanks and the others, they were relentless. Her property was the keystone to the whole area. The commission of this one deal alone would pay a lot of bills. Shanks said it all the time. Sign that land, and you've got your partnership. She's your aunt, Bennett, not mine. Now this. How was he going to tell them?

If he were only sure that he would inherit the house and land, he could tell Shanks to go to hell. But what if Addy changed her mind. What if she deeded the whole thing to that housekeeper, or to the city for a museum? He couldn't stop her. Then where would he be? He had to play it safe. Keep the law practice going. Cover his bases.

Addy had no idea how much trouble she was causing, sitting there on that gold mine property with her memories and her housekeeper. Gladys! That was another problem. What was her angle anyway? She had been in Addy's employ for what, maybe twenty-five or thirty years. What kind of person does that? Was she plotting to take it all? Angling for control? It happens all the time. You read about it in the papers. Some old fool kicks the bucket, and suddenly it's revealed that she changed her will, and it all goes to the caretaker, or the cat or something. He wouldn't put it past that lawyer of hers either. Grayson Chandler stood to gain a lot by making a deal with Gladys.

Lost in his rant, Edwin drove right past his building. He was two blocks down before he realized it. He turned right at the corner and circled back, glancing at his watch and cursing under his breath. He had twenty minutes to get his head together and make the meeting with the planning board. Addy had no idea!

CHAPTER 10

Mitchell Cavander was a man of few frivolous plea-
sures. Not that he couldn't afford them. As the founder
and president of a world-wide technology company,
he could afford any indulgence that he might desire,
but Mitchell Cavander was a serious man. He had
built his company by hand from the birth of computer
technology, and his mark was on every advancement.
He worked every day and drove his own domestic
sedan to his office. Most days, so that he could work
straight through, he carried his lunch. His frugality
was legend, and his focus on business unsurpassed. In
thirty-five fast-paced years he had dominated his chosen field of computer soft- ware and plowed his profits
into endless other businesses around the world. Now
in his sixties, he sat atop one of the great fortunes and
was counted among the five wealthiest billionaires in
the world.

He had a few diversions. Fencing was one, and
he worked at it dutifully in his private gym on the

grounds of his home in North Dallas. His other love was antique weapons, swords of all types and also firearms. His collection, kept out of sight except to a select few, was quite extensive. He loved the history of weapons, and his acquisitions reflected it. Beautifully designed, beautifully decorated, his weapons were among the most rare, and he could tell you the history and legend of each. Of particular interest in the last few years were American Civil War weapons. Mitchell tended to be obsessive like that, honing in on one period of time or one particular weapon until he had found it and possessed it.

And nothing pleased him more than stumbling on a find that no one else had discovered. So, as he leafed through the file of research on his latest interest, his juices were flowing. What a stroke of luck that he had happened on this mystery. One of those moments that could not be purchased for any price.

The door to his inner office opened quietly, and Murray Creed walked in. Mitchell didn't need to look up. He knew who it was. Only Creed had permission to enter this room, to look on this collection arranged in softly lit glass cases on all four walls. Any other person who passed through those doors would have to be personally escorted by Cavander, himself. "I want to move on this before anyone else gets interested in that house," he said.

Creed approached the table and glanced at the papers Cavender was studying. "How do you want to handle it?"

"Our offer to buy is still stalled, I suppose."

"This woman, Adeline Sinclair, she isn't easy to persuade."

Mitchell flipped through his research pages. "There are few details here." He tapped the folder with his index finger. "But, I'd bet good money that house is connected—the house, or somewhere on the grounds."

"Have you ever met her?"

"Once, at a fundraiser, years ago. Just in passing. Lovely woman, very proper. Could be one of my aunts." The two men exchanged a smile. "I see her point about the house. It's not practical, but I see her point." He sat down in a leather club chair, and Creed sat across from him. "Do we have any competition on this?"

"Several nibbles, one serious. Penrow has been very active in that area, but they have made very little headway with the Sinclair woman. I understand there might be one other company interested. I don't have any details yet."

"Who is representing Penrow?"

"Westfall & Rowe. They have a lot of the available downtown real estate under contract, I believe."

"So what is our edge?"

"Well, of course, we're still under contract to York, Wheeler & Shanks. I looked into their people, and it seems that Adeline Sinclair has a great nephew with the firm. Might be something."

Creed saw the spark in Mitchell's eyes. "Can we work with him?"

"I'm guessing we can. He's a junior partner, very ambitious."

"Great! Work it out. Let me know when you have a plan. We need to move on this. Barton & Ramsey is serious about the preservation thing, I'm sure. We need to be ahead of them."

Creed rose as his boss did and left the room. Mitchell turned back to admire his collection. He could see the perfect spot. It would take very little rearranging.

Dallas 1865

Paul Henri could hardly face his wife. He could barely stand to look into her eyes and see the pain. William, their son, their first born, was dead. Dead on a field of battle with a name they could scarcely pronounce. Dead almost two years before word came, and he died for a cause they could not embrace. The pain of knowing., of feeling he had somehow failed his boy by not stopping him from going, not imparting to him clearly his own beliefs in equality and peace, not convincing him that the reason they had come all this way to Texas was to avoid other people's wars, for not forbidding him to go, or making him stay well out of the fight. His grief was overwhelming.

And what of his part in this War Between the States? The Tucker and Sherrard Pistol Factory was in trouble, short on materials. Henri had been forced to use inferior metals to forge many of the pistols.

Often there was a shortage of parts altogether. The factory had slipped far behind schedule. The State of Texas had already delivered the gold payment that the Tuckers demanded instead of the nearly worthless Confederate money, and that had started a cry of protest in the Legislature. The Tuckers were accused of being less than loyal to the southern cause. Rumors circulated that they would be arrested and tried for treason, a hanging offense. So, without a word, the men had gone, on swift horses in the night, leaving Paul Henri in charge of the factory.

With the Confederacy crumbling around him, and daily rumors of Union invasion into East Texas, with a stack of undelivered guns and a payment in gold bars, he had to make a decision.

So he turned to his most loyal worker, Zebediah, the Tuckers' slave. A special bond had been formed between him and the man. Henri had never met a slave before, and Zebediah had never met a white man who treated him with a free man's respect. They worked side by side. Paul Henri was horrified by slavery, and Zebediah was his chance to do something about it. So the two men worked together, quietly and with growing respect, and formed a bond that the Tuckers could not dissuade or understand. Now, when Henri was struggling with maybe the most dangerous decision he had ever had to make, Zebediah was his choice.

The guns should never reach the soldiers. Paul feared that many of them were dangerous. The inferior metal might explode in the hand when fired. And besides, the Southern cause was all but lost. The Union had captured Vicksburg two years ago, and no supplies of any kind could reach the Confederate forces east of the Mississippi. The South was on its heels. Henri swore to himself that he would not contribute one more weapon that might take another life.

He would not remain party to the death of someone else's son. The guns could not be shipped.

The two men whispered, their heads close together. If the northern troops came, Henri knew he would be held accountable, arrested, maybe even shot. And if the Texans came looking for their guns and gold, he might be the one hanged. He told the slave his plight and asked the unthinkable. They had to hide the guns and payment. But if they were caught, if anyone suspected, they would be shot for hatching such a plot. Zebediah listened. He nodded. He understood. The danger, the grief, the desperation, he understood it all.

I know what to do, Boss," he whispered in return. "I'll take them out tonight. You don't need to worry 'bout where. I know just what to do."

CHAPTER 11

Dallas 2007

It was truly amazing the things people kept. Old receipts, gracious! So old that the paper was falling apart in her hands. Robyn handled everything carefully. It wasn't her job to clean the files, just search through for records.

She had been working for several weeks aided by a clerk from the office. Mary was a student intern working part-time. Nice girl, eager to help. Gladys had shown them the second floor study and then disappeared. So far, nothing. The only thing she knew for sure about Adeline's father and his father before him was, they were meticulous filers!

Old cancelled checks written in pencil. Counter checks where the person just picked one up in a store and wrote in the name of the bank. Robyn couldn't help but be amused.

It was a different time.

They were working their way through old file cabinets of papers, and so far they had found nothing older than 1932. It was going to be a slow process.

Gladys appeared at the study door carrying a tray. "Would you girls like to take a break and try some of this lemon cake I just got out of the oven?"

Robyn slumped back in her chair. "That sounds wonderful, Gladys. What do you say Mary? We'll blow off the diet today, you think?"

"Fine by me."

Gladys came in and sat the tray on a corner of the desk that Robyn hastily cleared.

"Adeline is down for a nap, right now, so I thought I'd just come join you up here for a while."

"Wonderful."

"I brought tea. Is that OK?" Robyn and Mary nodded. Gladys busied herself setting out the cake and pouring ice tea.

Interesting, Robyn thought. In all her times in the house, Gladys had never made an attempt at being sociable before. In fact, she had always been pretty stand-offish.

Gladys finished arranging and pulled up a chair. "I try to make one of these cakes ever so often for Adeline. It's one of her favorites."

Robyn took a bite. "Hmmm, I can see why. Very good!" Mary grined agreement with her mouth full, and Gladys nodded with pride.

"You've been providing favorites for Adeline for quite a long time, I take it."

"Yes, thirty-eight years, I think it is. And my mother worked for the Boll family when I was a little girl. I use to come along with her sometimes. Adeline and I go way back."

"That is so wonderful." Mary put in.

"She depends on you so much." Robyn said.

"Yes, well, I feel very protective of Addy. She's been like a second mother to me. When my husband, Hubert, got sick in '86, she paid all his medical bills. And she held my job for me while I took care of him until the end. I owe a lot to her."

"What a generous thing to do."

"And when I got sick with my stomach complaint two years ago, same thing. She took care of everything. I was laid up for three weeks."

Robyn just nodded. Gladys was leading up to something here. This was the most conversation she had ever heard from her.

"I'm telling you this by way of letting you know how I feel about Adeline. I ... I don't have much family. Hubert and I never had any children, and my mother and father are gone. Adeline is my family now. She has always been a wonderful person to work for, and I like this work, running this house. After Hubert died I was just at loose ends. And as Adeline has gotten older, I've taken over more personal things. I sold my house and moved in here after her first heart spell. I watch over her. Adeline seems stronger than she is, you know. She likes her independence, and I see that she has it. But she's fragile. I don't want anything to upset her in this."

"Upset her?"

"I know she loves this place, and I appreciate that you are trying to help her save it, but I worry." Gladys paused. Her blue eyes were sparkling with emotion. She pursed her lips as if to keep her words back.

"The only information Mary and I are looking for up here is pertaining to the house, Gladys. Any personal papers or family information, we will not touch. Any secrets are safe with us."

Gladys waved her hand to dismiss Robyn's words.

"Aw shaw! I don't care about family secrets. There's no secrets up here. I'm talking about her great nephew, Edwin Bennett. He's the problem. I don't want him threatening Addy over all this."

"Threatening? Has that happened?'

Gladys hugged her arms across her bosom. "Well, it sounded like it to me. And I don't think Adeline told you about it."

"No, she didn't."

He stormed out of here a few weeks ago, after she told him about the house and all, saying he would start legal action, or some such."

"What did Adeline say to that?'

"Nothing to Edwin. He was already gone. But she called her lawyer, Mr. Chandler."

"Good, that's the best thing to do."

"But today, this letter came." Gladys pulled a cream colored envelope out of her apron pocket. "I found it on the table after lunch. I saw Addy reading it and she was upset. I could tell. So when she went to lie down for a bit, I just took a peek."

She held the letter out to Robyn.

"Gladys, I can't read that. It's not my letter."

"Well, then I'll just tell you, because I'm afraid Addy won't. That rat is threatening to get her declared unfit and take over her affairs if she doesn't stop this historical designation thing." She stabbed her finger toward Robyn. "I'll not have that. Adeline has a heart condition. She doesn't need this. I was hoping if I told you, you could help her out. Maybe back off this business for a while, or something."

"I assure you, we'll do whatever is necessary to help Adeline," Robyn said. "Do you know if she has called her lawyer about this yet?"

"I don't think so. She was so upset, she just went straight to bed."

"Well, we've got to respond on this now if she is that upset." Robyn looked around at Mary. "Let's call it a day. You can take off a little early this afternoon, and I'll try to help Gladys figure this out."

"Tomorrow then?'

"Well, come to the office first, and we'll see where we are."

Gladys relaxed visibly when she realized Robyn was taking her seriously.

"Why don't you go check on Adeline. If she is awake, invite her to come down for some of this cake. I'll join you, and maybe she will share this with us, and we can ease her mind. Do you think that will work?"

"I'll do that right away." And Robyn saw the first smile she had ever received from Gladys Thornton.

"I'll come down and join you, and we can just chat for awhile. Give her a chance to tell us if she wants to. I promise to say nothing about our talk."

Gladys scurried out the door followed by Mary. Robyn began organizing the papers on the table. She needed to be able to keep things straight in case it was a while before she was here again.

CHAPTER 12

Gladys was hurriedly putting ice in the glasses when Robyn got to the kitchen. "She'll be right down. She was awake when I went to her room. The cake did the trick. Do you want tea or just water?"

"Water, please."

"Now, please don't tell her ..."

"I won't say a word. I promise."

"But, you need to ..."

They heard the whir of the elevator from the hall. Robyn reached out to touch Gladys' arm. "It will be fine. I promise. Let's just let her talk." Gladys smiled and nodded nervously.

"So, do I smell my favorite pound cake down here?" Addy appeared at the kitchen door.

"I thought you might like some today." Gladys glanced at Robyn.

"Well, it's a fine idea." Addy patted Robyn's shoulder as she sat down. "Good afternoon, dear. Are you making any progress up there?"

"One file at a time." Robyn helped her adjust her chair.

Gladys served the cake. "I just fixed you ice water."

"Thank you, dear. Tea this late in the afternoon, and I'll be up all night."

Gladys seated herself and made a show of concentrating on her piece of cake.

"I don't usually nap this long. I don't know what came over me today."

"Maybe it's the weather," Robyn suggested.

"Yes."

They ate in silence for a bit. Robyn studied Addy with a side-long glance. She look very tired, more fragile.

"I've been amazed at how meticulously your father and grandfather filed everything."

Addy laughed softly. "They were both very concerned with proper details, if I remember correctly. Mother always said both of them balanced their books to the penny and kept every receipt. I'm sure there is quite a mess up there."

"Not a mess. Like you say, very detailed, but not messy. I keep thinking we are going to find everything we need, though. I can't imagine that they didn't keep house records the same way."

"It's just finding them." Adeline smiled, and the three women fell silent again.

"Have you had any more thoughts on what you would like to see in your project?"

Addy looked at Robyn as though she was being called back from a far-off place. "No, I'll leave that part to you and Ramsey."

"What about your great nephew? Have you filled him in on our plan?"

Gladys' eyes went wide as she waited for Addy's response.

Addy took a deep breath and laid down her fork. She ducked her head for a moment. "My great nephew has his own plans, I think." She looked at Gladys. "Did you show her my letter?"

Gladys' mouth opened, but no sound came out. Addy reached across and patted her hand. "It's okay dear. I knew you would read the letter as soon as I realized I'd left it on the table. It can't stay a secret anyway." She looked at Robyn. "Mentally unfit. He didn't hold back, did he?"

"I haven't read it, Addy."

Adeline looked at Gladys, who, after a second, pulled the letter from her pocket and gave it to Robyn. Robyn read quickly down the page. Grave concerns for Adeline Sinclair's mental state ... Recommend medical evaluation." The phrases jumped out at her.

"Have you called your lawyer?" Robyn asked

"Not since the letter. I'll call directly. But don't let this influence you and your search."

"If it is going to cause you any stress, we can back off for a while until you address his accusations."

"No, I don't think that Grayson will advise that."

"Ramsey might talk to him, also. Ease his mind that we are not taking advantage of you."

Addy smiled. "Yes, I'm sure that is Edwin's only concern in this." Derision dripped from her words. She took a deep breath. "Don't worry, though. I think I still have one good fight left in me."

"What do you think Edwin's true concern is in this business?"

"Oh, he wants the money this land can bring. No

doubt about that. He's been very clear. And he wants the prestige of control. What he doesn't want is this house. He'll raze it to the ground before I'm cold in the grave, if he can."

"Is Edwin your only family?"

Basically. I'm afraid later generations in my family weren't very fruitful. He has two children. Other than that, it's distant cousins who have been out of contact for generations. My estate? It supports me, but not much more. Not enough to draw a crowd of relatives." She smiled. "This house and land. That's about all that's left." She laughed softly. "My financial planner didn't expect me to live this long, I guess, and neither did I."

"Well, between your Mr. Chandler and Ramsey, I'm sure they can placate Edwin. Let's let them handle that challenge."

"I agree. I'll go call Grayson right now." Addy rose from the table. "May I have my letter?"

Robyn handed it over, and Gladys blushed crimson, her eyes downcast.

"Thank you for the cake and for your concern." Addy said. "Both of you." She glanced first at Gladys and then at Robyn.

Gladys beamed.

They watched Adeline until she disappeared into the hall.

"Thank you!" Gladys whispered, as she cleared the dishes.

Robyn finished the last of her cake. Two pieces! What she didn't sacrifice for her job! She listened to the muffled phone conversation from the hall and waited until she heard Addy hang up and come back to the kitchen.

"Grayson asked you to tell Ramsey to call him at

his first opportunity. He's sending a boy over to get my letter."

"I'll go back to the office and fill Ramsey in right now."

CHAPTER 13

Robyn had been in Dallas for several months before she decided to make the leap and try to find her sister. She had intended to do it sooner, but then she stumbled onto the house and Adeline, and things had gotten very busy. She hadn't had time to think about Shelby. But now with all work on the house delayed, there were no more excuses. She had to track Shelby down. Every conversation she had with their mother, if it lasted long enough, finally drifted to the subject. "Have you gotten in touch? Have you found Shelby?" Why did her mother want to make contact so badly? Open those wounds again?

Shelby. Baby sister. The rebel. "Like my brother Robert," her father was given to saying in exasperation. Stubborn? Shelby could be the poster child for it.

For all Robyn's life she had heard, "Robyn, be patient with your little sister. She's not as big, as quick, as outgoing—supply your own adjective—as you." And as for Shelby herself. "Angry and rebellious right out of the womb," her mother might mutter. Angry at Robyn—Robyn's piece of cake is bigger—She got more presents—She always makes A's—Robyn always wins. A never-ending stream of complaints.

Robyn had spent the first eighteen years of her life apologizing to her little sister, trying to make it better to no avail. Now after all these years and all the peace and quiet, why drag up the relationship, she kept asking herself. And then in the back of her mind she heard her mother. "Have you talked to Shelby?"

The last address they had for her showed to be in an area called Deep Elm, pronounced El-um for some reason Robyn had not figured out. It was an area of night clubs and tattoo parlors popular with the young and the artsy. At least the tattoo artsy. Several of those new town house projects that Ramsey mentioned were changing the face of the area, but somehow Robyn knew that wasn't going to be Shelby's address.

Tucked in next to the new construction were old buildings in different stages of disrepair. The building that matched her address was a narrow doorway and stairs squeezed between two boarded-up store fronts. "Great! Wonderful neighborhood!" Robyn parked on the street and left her car with the uneasy feeling that it might not be there when she got back.

The battered street door resisted a little when she tried it. She stuck her head in the opening and peered up the stairs. She could hear a saxophone playing softly somewhere above her. That was encouraging. A row of six mailboxes just inside the door did not bear Shelby's name or number, but half the boxes had no markings at all, so that meant nothing. Robyn climbed the stair looking for number 203.

On the landing she caught her breath and got her bearings. Number 203 was the last door on the left.

She knocked and waited. The saxophone stopped and she heard shuffling behind the door. It opened a crack, and a black face with wire-rimmed round glasses peered through the slit.

"I'm looking for Shelby Jefferson. Is she still at this address?"

The man smiled and blinked his eyes. "Raven," he said.

"Pardon?"

"Raven, you're looking for Raven. She's on the roof."

Robyn stared back, then looked up as he pointed. "On the roof," he repeated. "Go on up. She's working." He pointed toward the window at the end of the hall. "Take the fire escape ladder."

Robyn looked out the window, then back at the door, but it was shut and the saxophone had started again.

The roof! Of course. Why not? This was perfect! Robyn studied the situation at the window, pulled off her shoes, hiked up her skirt, and hefted herself over the window sill onto the metal landing. Thank God the building was only two stories high. She climbed carefully up the rusted steps and peered out across the roof of the building.

There was someone up there all right, but from the back she would have never guessed it was Shelby. Dressed in solid black, combat boots and fishnet stockings, short cropped jet black hair with a shocking red streak across the top, the person was busy applying paint to a canvas and didn't hear her approach.

"Shelby?" Robyn called the name out when she was still some distance away, thinking that if she had the wrong person she could escape with a minimum of fuss. But when the person turned, she saw it was, in fact, her baby sister. Even under that mop of dyed hair and apparent pounds of mascara, it was still Shelby.

"For the love of God! What are you doing here?"

"Hello, Shelby. I didn't recognize you at first."

"That would be my plan, sis. What are you doing here?" she repeated.

"I live here now. I've taken a job here in Dallas."

"Christ! With the whole damn country to choose from, did you have to pick this town?"

"Well, it's a big city. I'm sure I won't crowd you too much."

Shelby let out a breath of exasperation and crossed her arms. "So. Mom sent you over to find me, I guess."

Robyn nodded. "She's worried. You doing all right?"

"Yeah, working, you know." Shelby gestured toward the canvas.

Robyn looked closer at the work. Not bad. Shocking colors, bold angry black stripes. It screamed Shelby. "I like it," she offered.

"No you don't." Shelby lit a cigarette, and they both laughed. She took time to inhale her first drag and blew out the smoke in a dramatic fashion. "Sorry to hear about the accident."

"Yes, well …"

"Sorry I didn't make it to the funeral, but …" Robyn waved her words away, "I wouldn't have known. I was unconscious for about four months. It wouldn't have mattered."

They fell silent for a time. Robyn looked out toward the city towers. "It's nice up here."

Shelby turned to study the view. "Yeah, my subject. I paint interpretive skylines. Turns out, people like them. There's a gallery down the street that will take as many as I can crank out."

"Hey, that's great."

"I'm not rich yet, but hey, who knows, right?"

"Right. … Who's the guy?"

"Huh? Oh, Jax. He's a musician. Pretty good. We've been together for while."

"Married?"

"No."

"So your name hasn't changed. I didn't see it on the mailboxes."

"Well, actually, it has changed. I'm not using Shelby any more. I just have one name. Raven."

"Raven, yes the … he said that. Jax called you that."

Shelby nodded. "Goes better with my brand."

Robyn frowned. "Your brand?"

"Yeah, to sell you have to brand yourself, you know. Set yourself apart. I tapped into the gothic craze with my skyline scapes. I put a little of my own blood into each painting." She held up a small glass vial she had hanging around her neck as a pendant. "That's my gimmick, and I sign them Raven."

"Clever."

Shelby smiled. "Whatever puts food on the table."

"Raven?"

"Yeah."

"Well, good for you."

"So, where are you working? Living?"

"Barton & Ramsey … architecture firm. I'm working on an old historic home over on Swiss Avenue right now. The Boll Mansion. I just found a place to live off Blackburn. I moved in a few weeks ago."

"Blackburn, my, my, the high rent district. I'm impressed."

"Well, it's close to work and I get a break on rent because Barton & Ramsey owns the building."

"You are the lucky one."

"Do you have a phone? We could exchange numbers."

"No. Haven't found the need."

"Well, can I give you my number?"

Shelby hesitated, then shrugged her shoulders. "Sure. Maybe I can still find a phone somewhere if I ever need it."

"I'll give you my new address, too." Robyn wrote her information down on a notepaper from her address book. "Well, I'll let you get back to your work."

Shelby took the paper and nodded.

"I'll tell Mom and Dad I saw you, and that you're doing great."

"Yeah, you do that."

"You could call them yourself, you know, or send a card. They worry, and they miss you."

Shelby raised her eyebrows. "Yeah, well, maybe I will one of these days, but you know, it just starts all over again."

Robyn smiled. No use to argue. "See you later." Robyn turned to go.

"See you around." Shelby called after her as she climbed down the ladder.

Robyn smiled when she heard that. For the first time ever maybe, she was coming away from an encounter with Shelby where she had not wound up apologizing for something. Will wonders never cease?

CHAPTER 14

After weeks of wrangling, the sit-down meeting with Edwin Bennett was finally scheduled for a Thursday morning. Ramsey went into the conference prepared for full battle. If setting the time was any indication of things to come, they were in for a war. Edwin had refused the first three meeting times offered to him because of his busy schedule. It was a power play on his part. He was following the old dueling rules. Never let your opponent select both the field and the weapon. In this case, Ramsey and Grayson agreed to let Edwin call all the shots. Whatever it took to get him there.

He arrived on time, though. Ramsey was a little surprised at that. Apparently Edwin had decided he already had the upper hand and didn't need any more concessions. They met at Grayson Chandler's office. Neutral ground of sorts. Handshakes all around. Grayson started them off.

"Thank you both for coming today. I know you have

busy schedules, but I think we can agree that Adeline Sinclair is a top priority for us all. We want to establish her interests and her wishes as soon as possible." He straightened the papers in front of him. "Now, Edwin, we have known one another a long time. You know I'm dedicated to Adeline. She has confided in me that you two are at cross purposes on this affair. Do you agree?"

"I just don't want my aunt to be taken advantage of." Edwin gave each man a quick glance. "That's my only concern in this." He rearranged himself in his chair.

"Certainly." Grayson continued. "Now Adeline has also confided in me that she wants to develop some way to preserve her house and possibly contribute something to the City of Dallas. Are you aware of this?"

"Very aware. That's why I'm concerned. I think she has been duped into thinking that if she signs over this property of hers, she can preserve it. I think someone is maneuvering to get control of her holdings, and I think they are not intending to give her full market value. In short, I think Mr. Ramsey here sees an opportunity to play on her emotions over that old house and walk away with some very valuable land."

Ramsey listened, with no reaction to the insult.

Grayson spoke in a calm tone. "Edwin, I don't think it's productive to start throwing around accusations in this."

Edwin sat back in his chair. "You're right. I'm just very concerned, and I need to hear what Mr. Ramsey has to say for himself."

Grayson and Edwin turned to look at Ramsey, who sat silent for a few moments letting the pause frame the moment.

"First off, Mr. Bennett, I would like to point out

that your Great Aunt Adeline Sinclair contacted me. I did not approach her first."

Edwin stiffened his posture, but he did not respond.

"Next," Ramsey shifted forward in his chair. "The plan being considered would not put your aunt's property in my hands, as you suggest. Barton & Ramsey will design the development, but we would not own or attempt to own any land or property in this arrangement. Adeline's estate would be hers to dispose of as she sees fit."

"By giving it away to the City of Dallas."

"I would say that is her choice."

"A ninety year old woman is not capable of making a decision like that. You are taking advantage of her age and frailty."

"So, you imply that Adeline isn't capable of managing her own financial affairs at this point?" Grayson asked.

"Obviously, if she is willing to give away a fortune in land like this."

"Well, that's what we're here to talk about today. What we want to do is establish what you see as the best plan of action. Compare it to the goals Mr. Ramsey's firm is offering and see if we can do something like Adeline has in mind. Do you agree?

Edwin's gaze snapped back and forth between the two men. "Right. I'm willing to listen."

"Fine. Now as Adeline's legal counsel, I'm going to ask something of you up front." Grayson paused for effect. "Your threat of legal action against her has been very stressful for Adeline. And I think we can all agree that in her advanced years, she does not need undue stress. Would you be willing to formally withdraw your threat in writing so that she can take that worry off her mind?"

Silence lasted for an uncomfortable amount of time.

"No, I won't do that. I think there is a real concern, and I won't do it."

"Possibly with the understanding that you can resubmit your request for control later if you need to. It will relieve Adeline's concern now, and get this partnership off on a positive note."

"Partnership?"

"Edwin, all three of us have only one true concern here. That's Adeline. Her doctor has indicated that with her heart history she does not need any undue stress. Her housekeeper is concerned. Will you withdraw your threat?"

Edwin smirked at the mention of Gladys, but he didn't comment.

Another long pause.

"With the understanding that I can press for control in the future if I see the need."

"Done. Now, if you'll sign this retraction letter." Grayson pushed the paper across the table. "It just states that you are retracting your first letter, and that you reserve the right to press your case in the future." Edwin read it quickly, signed the paper and tossed the pen back on the table.

All three men shifted in their chairs as though preparing for round two. Grayson quickly noted something on the paper before him. "Now, I've talked with Adeline at length. As you well know, Edwin, she is a very independent woman. I don't suppose a person gets to age ninety without a strong will." They all managed to smile at this. "She has a definite desire to see her home preserved in some way. And I think Mr. Ramsey will confirm that the house does have historic value."

"Yes," Ramsey interjected. "We have good reason

to believe that part of the house construction dates back to 1858. Were you aware of that?"

Edwin raised his eyebrows in surprise. "1858?"

"If the records and investigation prove what Adeline tells us, her house is possibly the oldest in the city, and could easily qualify for historic designation"

"Can that be proven?" Edwin folded his arms in a defensive pose.

"Yes, it can be, with records and with analysis of the building materials."

"So, in other words, the house could not be torn down."

"If it gains historic status, it's protected."

"Tying up a very valuable piece of real estate in a strategic area of growth." Edwin said.

"That's where our planning comes in," Ramsey said. "It depends on how the house is preserved, and how the surrounding land is used."

"Wasted space." Edwin said.

"There are several other companies and partnerships that are interested in the area. I think we need to survey what plans have been put in place for those properties. Would you agree to that?"

Edwin nodded. "My law firm represents several of those companies right now. But the other land has been sold to developers for fair market value. Not given away."

"So, if your Aunt were selling the property, you would not contest it."

"No. That's what I have suggested to her. Sell on the condition that nothing is done as long as she is alive. The deal would be done. The money guaranteed, and she would not be disturbed."

"The one thing wrong with that plan is that in the end, Adeline's house is destroyed."

Edwin shrugged his shoulders. "Then make me a better offer."

"Make you an offer?"

Meaning my great aunt and me. Make us an offer. As her closest relative, I need to be party to any plans, and then, of course, I would naturally negotiate the contract through my company, York, Wheeler & Shanks."

"What if … ," Grayson leaned back in his chair, "we could work out a plan where Adeline receives fair market value and still preserves the house and grounds?"

Edwin laughed and shrugged his shoulders. "And you can do all this?"

"I can try. Would you be in agreement if we can deliver?"

Long pause. Again Edwin's gaze darted back and forth between the two men. "Fair market value?"

Grayson nodded.

Edwin drummed his fingers on the table. "And I reserve my right to protest this in the future."

"Agreed."

"Done. Do you have a time frame to produce this miracle of yours?"

"Don't tie me down." Grayson raised his hands in a surrender pose. Just give us some time, and I'll get back with you. In the meantime, Ramsey and his office will continue their research of the property."

"On the condition that nothing can be formally agreed without my approval."

"Done." Grayson stood up from his desk. "So at this point, we'll all stand down and let Barton & Ramsey research the property before any other action is taken. Agreed?"

Edwin nodded and stood up to shake Grayson's

extended hand. Ramsey waited his turn. "I'll keep in touch through Grayson, here."

"Fine," Edwin left the room in a hurried step. Ramsey and Grayson watched him as far as the elevator.

"We've got some homework to do, I think."

"I'll get on tracking down any other developers in the area."

"I'll get back on the project plan. Give me a call when you have some names for me so we can check out the competition."

CHAPTER 15

Edwin Bennett left Grayson Chandler's office with a sense of confidence. So what if he had retracted his letter threatening to take action against Adeline? The letter had gotten results. People were listening to him now. Chandler might think he can pull off this miracle deal to save the house, but now it didn't matter so much. As long as the land sold for fair market value, and he got to negotiate the contract, the pressure from Shanks would be off his back. He didn't really care what happened to that old mausoleum. And even though Addy couldn't see it now, he was doing both of them a favor. Besides, if it worked out and the land did sell, and the will was in his favor, he could tell them all to go to hell.

His cell phone rang as he walked to the parking lot. He checked the number; unknown. "Hello?"

"Edwin Bennett?

"Yes, who is this?"

"Murray Creed, Mr. Bennett. I represent Vander Corporation.

Edwin was immediately attentive. "Yes."

"I wonder if I might have a little of your time this afternoon? I think we might have a common interest."

"Certainly. Ah …"

"Say, 2:00. You know our office address, I assume."

"Yes, yes I do."

"Fine, ask for me at the front desk, and someone will direct you. I'll alert the guard." The line went dead.

Murray Creed! Vander Corporation! The third largest company in the U.S. The corporation had its finger in every field from high tech to pork bellies. Mitchell Cavander made the list of top ten billionaires every year. Should he go home and change? He looked down at his suit. No, don't try too hard. He was fine. Maybe just a fresh shirt and get his jacket pressed before he went. Murray Creed! Unbelievable! Grab some lunch. Check his calls. He found his car and sped down Main.

⁂

Chandler called Adeline as soon as Ramsey left his office.

"Thank you, Grayson. That is a great weight lifted." Adeline said. "At least I know the white coats aren't coming for me today."

Grayson laughed at her joke. "Actually Edwin was quite straightforward in the meeting. His main concern, he says, is your well being."

"Yes, I'm sure that it is."

Grayson chuckled at the incredulous tone in her voice. "At least he has agreed to stand back and let

Barton & Ramsey do their appraisal. We can't discount him, but as for now, he isn't the enemy."

"So, what happens next?"

"I'm sure the researchers will be back in the next few days. Then we wait to see what they uncover. Dalton Ramsey will be in touch."

"Well, you've come to my rescue again. Thank you, Grayson."

"No problem. That's why I'm here. Is there anything else I can do?"

"As a matter of fact, there is. It's rather silly, I guess, but if you'll indulge me, I'll be very grateful."

"Anything. What do you need?"

"Harriet Campbell was visiting her niece in Houston recently ..."

"How is Harriet? I haven't talked with her in years."

"She's fine. Busy as ever and maybe a little confused. I don't know. Anyway, Harriet tells me she saw my name in the obituaries down there in The Houston Post."

"Whoa! That would be a shock!"

"Yes, well, she was very upset. I tried to pass it off as a strange coincidence, or even a mistake, but she was sure she saw it. The description she read to me. Well, it was very strange. I was wondering. Do you have the resources to check that out for me? Find out if the name was a mistake, and if not, who the person was?"

"I certainly do. I'll be glad to check. Give me the name as she saw it."

"Mrs. Albert Sinclair."

"And the date she saw the paper?"

"It was the second week of February."

"So, that would make it ... the week of the 6th." I'll put someone on that and get back to you"

"And Grayson ... , you must promise to be completely honest with me. No matter what."

"Always, Adeline, always."

CHAPTER 16

The office tower of Vander Corporation was worthy of its reputation. Edwin tried not to gawk at the grandeur in the lobby, but it was hard. Marble everywhere, gold fixtures, magnificent chandeliers, but the guard at the desk didn't seem to notice him looking around.

"I'm here to see Murray Creed. I have an appointment."

"Name?"

"Edwin Bennett."

"May I see some identification, please."

"Certainly," He fumbled for his driver's license. The guard studied his photo and then him. "Yes, sir. Take the third elevator. The receptionist there will direct you."

Inside the elevator he realized it was an express directly to the thirty-second floor. Very impressive. He straightened his tie and checked his image in the brass door reflection to see that his hair hadn't been ruffled by the wind in the street. When he stepped off the elevator, the woman at the reception desk was smiling. "Good afternoon, Mr. Bennett. They are waiting for you in Mr. Cavander's office." She motioned for him to follow her.

Cavander's office! The words hit him like an electric shock. He struggled to maintain his composure. Cavander's office! The floor changed from marble to plush carpet.

When he entered the room, Edwin's first impression was that there was no one there. No one behind the impressive desk, anyway, but to his right, Murray Creed stood up slowly from a seating area by a huge picture window. Edwin recognized him from newspaper photos he had seen.

"Mr. Bennett, thank you for coming on such short notice. I'm Murray Creed." They shook hands. "I'd like to introduce you to my boss, Mr. Mitchell Cavander."

Cavander rose slowly from a large leather sofa as Edwin moved to shake his hand, also. "Thank you for coming today, Mr. Bennett" His grip was vice- like.

"My pleasure," he managed to say. Edwin's thoughts were spinning. The two men looked like a matched set. Mitchell Cavander was slightly taller and slimmer, maybe, but both men were short, very short. Surprisingly so. He towered over both of them. It made him self-conscious.

"Have a seat." Creed indicated another club chair in the grouping.

Edwin sat down quickly as the two men settled back into their chairs. Now they were at the same level.

Edwin's heart was racing. Mitchell Cavander! I don't believe this! He gave him a quick glance, then back to Creed.

"We thought we would sit over here where it's a

little less formal." Creed said. "Quite a view isn't it?" He nodded toward the window.

Edwin looked out over the towers of downtown Dallas. "Yes, very impressive."

Creed leaned forward slightly. "I suppose you are wondering about the nature of this meeting."

"Yes, well ..."

"You're with York, Wheeler & Shanks I understand." Cavander broke in.

"Yes."

"Specializing in commercial real estate law." Creed spoke up.

"For the most part."

You're a junior partner there. Is that right?" Cavander asked.

"Yes, that's correct, but ..."

"I'll have to have a word with York about that. He's overlooking a talent."

Edwin's glance darted between the men again. Was he being played here? He felt like a mouse between two cats.

"Mr. Bennett, or may I call you Edwin?" Cavander said.

"Certainly."

"Are you a history buff, Edwin?"

"Yes, I read it quite a lot. Texas history mostly."

"Ah yes, me too. There's some good books out there. I guess T. R. Fehrenbach's Lone Star is the best over-all history."

"I agree."

"Course, I love J. Frank Dobie. All of his books are good." My favorite is *Coronado's Children*."

"*Vaquero of the Brush Country* would be mine."

"Yes, that's a good one, too. They all have stood the

test of time, I think." Cavander laughed softly. "I guess I'm dating myself though. There are some more recent books that I could recommend as well. We understand you are well connected to Texas history yourself. One of the old Dallas families, I believe."

"Yes, on my mother's side. Her great-great- grandfather was Henry Boll."

"Quite right. One of the La Reunion colonists."

"Yes."

"I've gotten interested in the colony recently." Cavander said. "I bought some old buildings in Lancaster, out south of here. Do you know anything about that area?"

"No, no, I don't."

"Some of the La Reunion colonists moved there, too, just as your ancestor moved to Dallas."

"Ah."

"Man over there was named Paul Henri. Ever heard of him?"

"No, I haven't." Edwin shifted uneasily in his chair. Where was this going?

"He was an associate of your great-great-great-grandfather Henry Boll. Both were successful businessmen in their later years."

"I understand my ancestor was in real estate, like me." Edwin took a deep breath and glanced at Creed again.

"Yes," Cavander said. "Paul Henri was an engraver by trade, but in Lancaster he was a business man; general store, banking, that sort of thing."

Cavander reached to pour a glass of ice water from a crystal decanter on the table. He handed a glass to Edwin. Caught by surprise, Edwin quickly reached to accept it.

Cavander continued, "Among the buildings I

acquired in Lancaster I found a mass of Henri's records. Very interesting. The building had been part of an old gun factory during the Civil War. Paul Henri was employed by the Confederacy to make pistols there. Have you heard of this before?"

"No, I haven't." Edwin took a sip of water, then wondered if he could just set it down. Unsure, he just held it carefully in both hands.

"In his papers I found some old journals that Henri apparently kept from time to time. He mentions your ancestor Henry Boll quite often."

"Really."

"Apparently they were close friends."

"Well, if they came over to this country at the same time, maybe ..."

"That's what I thought." Cavander leaned forward slowly. "I was hoping you might be able to help me out on this"

"In what way?"

"Well," Cavander glanced at Murray Creed. "I'm interested in finding out if your ancestor kept any records himself. Maybe your records and mine would blend together, fill in some gaps."

"Gaps?"

"It's rather complicated. Too detailed to go into now, but let's just say, I would be very grateful if you could help me out."

"I still don't understand exactly ..."

"Do you have access to your family papers? That is to say, the papers of Henry Boll?"

"No, no, I've never gotten into the whole family history thing." Edwin laughed nervously, but the two men didn't join him. The water glass felt as though it weighed ten pounds in his hands.

"That's unfortunate, Edwin, because genealogy can

be very interesting ... and lucrative, I might add."

"Lucrative?"

"For instance, if you could find the papers I'm interested in, I would be willing to compensate you for your trouble."

Edwin sat in puzzled silence while the two men stared at him. "For paper, just records?" He said, when he recovered his voice.

"Journals, receipts, that type thing, for the years 1862 through 1868."

"I'd have no idea where to look for something like that."

"That would be your decision."

"Researchers are there now, looking for the records on the house."

"I'm aware of that. That's not what I need. My search will not interfere with Barton & Ramsey."

"Well, I'd have to clear it with Adeline."

"It would be best if you kept my name out of it. Vander Corporation is negotiating to buy your aunt's property through the proper channels. Through your company, in fact. But this search would be a private matter just between us. As compensation for your help, we would naturally ask your company to put you in charge of our account with your firm."

Again Edwin was shocked into silence. Their account? The Vander account was worth millions to whoever handled it. Millions and a full partnership.

"I can see you are a little surprised by our offer." Creed said. "Why don't you take a little time to think about it and get back to us." He rose and gestured to Edwin to do the same.

"Yes," Edwin managed to say. He fumbled to set his glass down and shook hands with both men.

"When do you think you might have our information?"

Edwin hesitated. "I ... , I don't know. I ..."

"Let's just say we trust you'll act on this as soon as possible. Would that be satisfactory?"

"Yes, I think so."

"Good, good. Thank you for coming today." Cavander patted him on the shoulder as they walked to the door. "I'll look forward to hearing from you."

Cavander stopped at his office door, but Creed walked Edwin to the elevator. "I can't emphasize enough how interested Mr. Cavander is in these records. I think you might be looking at a very bright future if this can be worked out. I would caution though, that time is at a premium. I would think you should have this all tied up in no more than two weeks. Or, of course, Mr. Cavander could look for other sources."

As the door on the elevator closed, Edwin managed to say, "Yes, thank you."

The ride down and the walk to his car was a blur. What had just happened? An offer to become Mitchell Cavander's real estate law consultant? He felt like lightning had just struck him. A word from Cavander was like gold in this town. He would be set for life.

And the records he talked about. They could easily be somewhere in that old house. Lord knows Addy never threw anything away. But finding them quickly. And finding them without explaining it all to her. That was going to take some planning.

CHAPTER 17

Robyn knocked on the door at 203, waited, and then knocked again. This time no saxophone played. She even crawled out on the fire escape and climbed to the roof, but no "Raven" was up there painting. After a frustrating thirty minutes of trying to decide her next move, she wrote out yet another note on a sheet from her organizer and added it to the collection already on the apartment door. It was the best she could do under the circumstances. But if Shelby let her down on this, she was going to give her a serious piece of her mind! Their parents' plane was landing in less than two hours. Shelby better make a showing. That was all she could say. This was her fourth trip over here in the last week. She had found no one each time, and her notes had gone unanswered. She hadn't even been able to find anyone to ask if they had moved or something, not even that art dealer Shelby had mentioned. Robyn stomped back to her car and drove away in a huff.

It would break her parents' hearts if Shelby refused

to see them. She would have to make up some sort of excuse. She navigated the one way streets back toward the freeway ... hell, what was she thinking. They've already heard all the excuses. They knew the score. You can not fix this, my dear. It's not your job in life to control your sister!

Her parents probably didn't even expect to see Shelby, if the truth be told. She looked at her watch. There was just enough time to make the drive to D-FW airport to meet the plane. She slipped into traffic on the freeway and threaded her way to the correct lane.

This was going to be a good weekend. She was determined. She could show off her apartment, take them by the office and by the house. They would be pleased and impressed and thrilled for her, she knew. Her parents would handle the Shelby thing. They had done it many times before. They would make a few excuses and pretend it didn't matter.

But she could strangle her baby sister for putting them through this again and again. If they would just give up on her. Of course, Robyn knew that would never happen. And unfortunately, Shelby knew it too. Daddy would say nothing, and Mom would smooth the whole thing over. Well, whatever! The three of them would have a fun time.

Her cell phone rang as she entered the airport toll-gate. It was her mother. Their plane was early. They were at baggage pickup. Robyn assured them she would be right outside the doors when they walked out of the terminal. Her new Honda was white. Be looking for her.

She navigated the maze of lanes without a bobble,

and when she rounded the turn on the arrival level there they stood smiling and waving. Robyn jumped out for a quick hug and helped her dad put the luggage in the trunk. They were in the car and rolling in no time.

"Gosh, you guys look great! Was it a good flight?"

"Yep, got the bulkhead seat so I had some leg room," her father said.

"The plane was packed! Everyone had carry-on luggage. It was a sight. Some of those bags were huge! Your father had trouble finding an overhead bin for ours."

"Isn't that always a hassle?" Robyn maneuvered her way through traffic. "But I'm so glad you're here!"

"Is Shelby meeting us somewhere?"

"I don't know, Mom. I've been trying to get in touch ever since I knew you were coming. They must be out of town or something. But I left a note for her. Hopefully she'll get the message while you are here."

In the rearview mirror she could see the shrug of her father's shoulders and the mask of disappointment and disgust settle for a moment on his face, but beside her she heard her mother chant her usual. "Well, I'm sure she's busy. She'll come by if she can."

"I was thinking Italian tonight, if that's all right. There's a good place near my apartment."

"Sounds good." Her father's smile was back. "We had some sort of little old sandwich at the airport in Atlanta. I could do with some good pasta."

⚬⚬⚬✕⚬✕⚬✕⚬⚬⚬

Shelby never showed. The three of them had a great visit. Robyn showed off her new apartment and her new office. They toured the Dallas Museum of Art and the Nasher Sculpture Garden, drove around the city and saw spots Robyn had never had time to see herself. They had lunch at the Dallas Arboretum and walked around the gardens. She drove by the Boll house and told them about the history.

By Sunday night they were so exhausted from all the walking, they decided to order Chinese and stay in. Her father found something to watch on her new TV. Robyn and her mother found a spot on the balcony and tried out her new patio chairs.

"So, have you met many interesting people here?" Mom cut right to the chase.

Robyn smiled. "I've been covered up at work since my first day. Outside of that I haven't really met any-one."

"Well, I hope that changes. You need to reach out. Are you going to church? That's always a good way to meet …"

"Mom." Her mother paused. "Please, let's not go into the 'are-you-seeing-anyone' conversation."

"Well, are you?"

"No."

"Robyn, you can't keep hiding. You're young. You have your whole life ahead of you. You …"

"I'm not ready! Please, no lectures. I'm not inter-ested."

"Very well." They stared out across the skyline and listened to distant voices from a park across the way.

"How far away does Shelby live from here?"

"Not far, but …" Robyn glanced at her mother and saw that determined glint in her eye.

"… but it would be a bad idea to just drop in. She's out of town. Her friend is a musician. They're prob-ably on tour or something."

"Is the friend male or female?"

"Male, a saxophone player. I only spoke with him briefly. Seemed nice enough. Sort of 'out there,' like Shelby." They both laughed softly.

"Well, that's good. With Shelby, you never know."

"He's black, by the way. I'll just get that out of the way."

Her mother smiled. "Well, as long as she is happy. If he's a good man, that's all that counts."

Robyn smiled. Her mother. Any liberal pundit in the country would quickly assume her mother should be a racial bigot. She was a southern girl through and through, and the honey dialect of Atlanta dripped from her every word. But if there was one thing she and Daddy had drummed into their heads from birth, it was racial equality; to treat everyone with respect. Stereotypes don't always fit.

"Maybe he can settle Shelby down a little," her mother added.

Robyn didn't respond, but to herself she was thinking, a jazz musician and a counter-culture artist. I doubt it.

They gazed out across the city, each lost in their own thoughts. After a bit her mother spoke.

"So tell me more about this little lady you are working with. Adeline, did you say?"

"Yes. Adeline Boll Sinclair. She is ninety years young, sharp as a tack, and full of life. You would just love her, Mom. I fell in love with her house the first time I saw it. And my first thought was that you would love this place. I didn't want to intrude this weekend, but the next time you come, I'll take you on a tour."

"Is it like our house?"

"In some ways. It's quite a bit larger than ours. The central structure was built in 1858, if you can believe it, and the rest added later. That's old for this part of the country. Dallas wasn't even established until the mid 1850s. Most of the rooms were built on in 1889, and the library was added in 1924. I'm researching the building with plans to seek historical designation. Barton & Ramsey is working on development of the surrounding land."

"That sounds wonderful. But don't let your work take over your life. You need to get out and meet some young people. You can't work all the time."

Robyn just smiled. Mom and her agenda could not be denied. Better to just agree. "I'll work on it, Mom, I promise. ... I'm so glad you and Dad came out to see me." The redirection worked.

"Yes, it's been great. And you can come this summer. Is that right?"

"I'll surely try."

"And maybe Shelby and her friend can come with you."

"It's worth a try, I guess." She kissed her mother on the forehead. "We better get to sleep. Your flight is at eight tomorrow. We'll have to leave here by six."

"Yes. Let's go wake your father up and get him to bed."

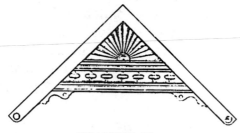

CHAPTER 18

When she got to the office on Monday morning Ramsey was waiting for her.

"You're on again. Edwin Bennett signed a letter retracting his threat and promised not to get in the way of our research."

Robyn bristled. "Well, that is just really nice of him, since he has absolutely no right to tell Addy what to do about anything."

Ramsey laughed softly. "Well, he seems to think so, and I'm thinking it's best we placate him until we have our paperwork in place."

"Right."

"So, you can get back into your search as soon as you please."

"I'll go back this afternoon if it's all right with Adeline"

"Happy hunting."

Robyn found everything just as she had left it when she had stopped the search. Looking around at the stacks of files and other cabinets yet untouched it seemed she had barely scratched the surface. Rather overwhelming, actually. But Mary would be back tomorrow and another pair of hands would help. She sat down at the desk and attacked the stack of papers in front of her. Item by item lists of purchases. Who keeps all this stuff?

Adeline appeared at the door. "Busy again?"

"Yes, well about to be. How are you this morning?" Robyn relaxed back in her chair. "Come in."

"I don't want to interrupt. Just wanted to welcome you back."

"I haven't even started yet." Robyn got up and cleared a chair next to her desk.

Adeline sat down and looked around the room. "I haven't been in here in awhile." Her gaze stopped at a small table by the windows. "My desk," she pointed, "I learned to write at that desk." She smiled. "I would sit there while my grandfather worked. He would give me sentences to copy."

"Do you remember your grandfather well?"

"Oh yes, I was seven when he died. He was seventy-two and in good health until the last. He was very proper. Always wore a tie and jacket." Adeline smiled. "Even in summer with no air conditioning. I don't know how they did it."

"I can't imagine." Robyn said.

"I came up to invite you to lunch today. Gladys is making a chicken pie and one of my favorite cakes."

"Thank you, that sounds wonderful."

"That's my favorite meal." Adeline smiled. "It's my birthday today. Ninety-one years. Isn't that something?"

"Oh, I'm so sorry I didn't realize."

"No, I made Gladys promise not to tell. I don't like a fuss anymore. But I do love Gladys' chicken pie. Please come."

"Yes, I'd love to."

"Wonderful." She smiled and gave Robyn a wink as she pulled an envelope from her pocket. "I found something I think might be of help." She handed it to Robyn and motioned for her to open it. It was photos, some of them old tin types. Most of them were of the house.

"Oh, these are wonderful!"

"That tin type is my grandfather and the next one is my grandmother. The next one is of my grandparents out on the front step. Notice there are no bushes around the place. I think that was made not long after the house was built."

"My, look at the elaborate beading work on the veranda railing. That's not there anymore."

"No, I think there was a storm years later, and a lot of the trim was damaged. Papa just had the workmen simplify it a little. They left it off."

"Other than that, there haven't been many changes across the front, have there?"

"No," Adeline studied the picture. "Only the color. It was lavender."

"The veranda?"

Adeline nodded. "With white trim."

"Lavender." Robyn repeated.

"The next photograph was made years later in the '20s. My father's new roadster is out front." Adeline pointed at the picture. "You can see the library wing in the background there. That's my father with his foot on the running board and my mother next to him."

"The trees and bushes have grown a little."

"There are a few others there. I couldn't find anything of the original place. I'm sorry."

"No, these are wonderful. They'll be a big help in the restoration. Thank you."

The last photograph was a more modern type, probably the 1950s, Robyn guessed. It was Adeline and a man standing on the veranda. They were both smiling and he had his arm around Adeline's waist.

When Addy saw the picture she reached for it. "Oh, how did that get in there?"

"Who is that?"

" Just an old friend"

"Aw, now. Come on," Robyn teased. "He looks like more than just a friend."

Adeline looked at the photo for a moment, then stuffed it away in her pocket. "Well." She smiled. "His name was Walter Hayley. He courted me for a while."

"What happened to him?"

"I heard that he passed away about five years ago. He was living in Seattle at the time."

"So, you kept in contact all these years?"

"No, a mutual friend told me. Walter and I hadn't spoken in fifty years, I guess."

"I wondered about that." Robyn leaned back in her chair. "Why didn't you ever remarry, Addy?" You must have had offers."

Adeline gave Robyn a side-long glance over the top of her glasses, "'Young lady, you ask too many questions."

"Now, come on. I'm your new best friend, remember? We're supposed to share secrets."

Adeline laughed. "Gracious, … well, yes, I did have several proposals after Albert was killed, but Walter is the only one I ever seriously considered."

"So?"

"He planned to move away. I just couldn't do that. If he would have stayed here in Dallas, then ... but I just couldn't go. I felt a duty, I guess."

"A duty?"

"To Albert and to his memory ... , and to my family. My purpose was here. If I had gone with Walter, ... things happen for the best, I think."

Robyn bit her lip to keep from saying what she was thinking. Adeline didn't need to be second guessed.

Adeline patted her hand. "You should understand. When you have given your heart to someone, it is a lifetime trust."

An image of Jonathon's face flashed across Robyn's mind. She felt a jolt as if something had struck her. There was a roaring in her ears. "Yes," she said.

Unaware of the effect of her words, Adeline rose slowly. "Well, I'll let you get back to work. "We'll call you for lunch. Gladys always does something special for me."

"Yes, that sounds wonderful. Just let me know when you are ready," Robyn managed to say. Get control, girl. No time for tears here. Get control.

She watched Adeline leave the room. Her step rather halting today. A duty, she had said. A duty to her memories. Is that what she was carrying, also? Up to now she had been concentrating on just making it from one day to the next. Any thought of the rest of her life she couldn't handle. Years she had been robbed of, without Jonathon, without the baby. Her vision clouded over with tears. How could she stop it, stop feeling married, stop feeling like a mother-to-be? The last thing she wanted was ... what? To be alone? But ... she couldn't deal with this now. She pushed away the thoughts and tackled the files before her. Think about the house.

Edwin Bennett sat at his desk and stared at the papers before him without seeing them. His mind was racing. Legal consultant for Vander Corporation. The title kept flashing in his mind. Consultant. It was too good to be true, and yet it was. He had heard it from Cavander's own lips, but there were conditions. He had to find the files. He was being used he knew, but so what! Cavander might think he was putting something over on him by blindsiding him with this big offer, but he was no fool. He knew the way deals were done—how much "who you know" could affect opportunity. His family ties—just the edge he needed to snag a prime position like this. He would be crazy to let this slip away. And Cavander had emphasized that his interest would not interfere with Addy's plans for the house. So what was the harm? But now, the problem; how to find those files.

He could simply ask Aunt Addy, but what if she refused? That was out of the question. He could demand to review all the papers that Barton & Ramsey had seen so far, but that would raise too much suspicion. Cavender wanted this kept quiet. So what was left? Time to use your wits, old boy. He dialed the phone and took a deep breath.

Adeline answered.

"Hello, Aunt Addy, Happy Birthday!" He winced at his cherry tone. Too much. Play it cool.

"Thank you, Edwin. I didn't think you would remember this year." Her voice sounded less than thrilled to hear from him.

"No, I couldn't forget your day." There was an awkward silence. "I wanted to check on you and see how your house project was progressing." Edwin's voice relaxed into a calm counselor's tone. "I suppose you have talked with Grayson Chandler."

"Yes, he tells me you have worked out your opposition to the research."

"Well, I felt much better once Dalton Ramsey assured me he was acting in your best interest and not pressuring you."

"Pressuring?"

"Adeline, I think it would be wonderful to preserve the house. You know that. I just want you to be treated fairly. It's my only concern."

There was a slight pause before Adeline replied. "And Grayson tells me you have retracted your threat to have me ruled incompetent."

"Incompetent? No, Adeline, that was just a grave misunderstanding. I never meant to imply ... I was only serving notice to anyone involved that I would be watching over your interest with you. I never intended that letter to come across as a threat to you." Edwin squirmed in his chair. This was not going well.

"Yes, well, thank you for your withdrawal."

Try a different tack. "And when I heard from Dalton Ramsey that the house very well does have historic value ... I mean the 1850s. That's amazing. I never realized."

"Yes." The line fell silent again.

"I guess I need to be paying more attention." Edwin laughed. "That's quite impressive."

More silence.

"The reason I called today is, I would like to try and make all this up to you, if I can. We can start over fresh, I hope. I'd love to get involved, like you suggested before, to come out and let you walk me through all this. It sounds fascinating, and I've never really gotten into the family story before." Edwin held his breath.

More silence. "I suppose that might be good," Adeline finally answered.

"What I'm thinking is, I'd take the afternoon off tomorrow and spend it with you. Maybe take a tour of the house with you. Spend some time …"

"I wouldn't want to disturb Robyn."

"Robyn?"

"The young lady researching for Barton & Ramsey."

"Oh, I'd love to meet her."

"Really"

"Yes, I got the impression from Dalton Ramsey and Grayson that you two have made quite a connection. So how about I plan to come tomorrow, and you can give me a family history lesson?"

More silence. "Very well, I'll see you tomorrow. Robyn and her helper usually get here about nine. Any time after that should be fine."

"Great! I'll clear my desk in the morning and come out about 1:00. See you then."

Edwin dropped the phone back in the cradle and slumped in his chair. His heart was racing with an adrenalin rush. He felt like he had just survived a fight. That little old woman was something else! But, it had worked. He was in. He could do this.

CHAPTER 19

Robyn made one more effort to contact Shelby. And the whole time she was fussing at herself, arguing really. Her practical side kept counseling "Let it go. Don't waste your time." But her emotional side pushed the logic away. She just wanted to see Shelby's face when she confronted her about missing their parents' visit. Just get her reaction. It would tell a lot. A look of disappointment? Not likely, knowing how closed off Shelby was, but a smirk of triumph? That would tell her all she needed to know. Tell her that Shelby was intent on punishing her parents for some imagined slight. Tell her not to bother, not to play to her sister's selfishness anymore, regardless of what her mother dreamed of.

But there was still no answer at Shelby's door, and the notes were still hanging there like bandages on the battered wood. Either Shelby had ignored them, or never seen them. So now the ball was in her court. If she called, she called.

Robyn walked away down the dingy stairs and out past the graffiti-scrawled boarded-up windows. There was a new notice posted across the wood announcing demolition of the building. All occupants must vacate by the end of the month. Very well, Shelby could disappear again if she chose. It was up to her.

Edwin showed up promptly at 1:00, just as he had said. Adeline answered the door. No reason to involve Gladys. She could sense a difference immediately. Edwin was smiling for one thing. He had removed his tie and jacket for another. He looked a little less stuffy.

"Good afternoon, Aunt Addy. Happy birthday." He handed her a vase of tulips.

"Thank you, Edwin. How thoughtful."

"One day late, but ..." He laughed nervously.

"They're lovely. I'll just set them here on the entry table."

They both studied the flowers for a moment. "So," Edwin clapped his hands together. "I'm ready for my history lesson. Where do we start?" He looked around the entry hall as if he had never seen it before.

Adeline studied him for a moment. "I'm glad to see you are interested, Edwin."

"Yes, well, it's about time, isn't it?" Edwin glanced around the entry again. "Is this part of the older house?"

"No." Adeline followed his gaze. "This is the new part ..." She led the way across the entry hall. "Back here, this part is older. The old house is the music room."

Edwin placed his hand on the limestone wall. "How old did you say?"

"1858 is when Henry Boll started building it. Do you know about the colony?"

"A little. It was over across the Trinity, wasn't it?"

"Out where the bulk mail center is today, along Interstate 30."

"Yes, our firm handled that deal, I think. It was before I joined, but there's lots of industrial acres out there." He surveyed the room again. "So Henry Boll would be my great-great-great grandfather. Is that right?"

"Yes. He was a butcher by trade. He and a Mr. Nussbaumer left the colony at the same time, and your ancestor worked at the Nussbaumer shop in the beginning.

"I understood that he was in real estate, like me."

"Well, as an older man. That happened sort of by accident really. The farm that he originally bought here grew in value over the years, so he began to sell it off for development." She made a turning motion with her hand. "It was a matter of being in the right place at the right time, I think."

"Amazing. It's hard to imagine Dallas as a small village like that."

"And this land was on the outskirts of the town, several miles out, actually."

"What a wonderful time to have lived. The deals that were made ..."

"The road out here in front was called Swiss Road because it ran from town out to these farms. Nussbaumer's house was just across the street there. When they incorporated all this into the city of Dallas, they named the road Swiss Avenue."

"How much land did we have here at the house?"

"Probably a section, about 600 acres, I think."

"Wow, think of the value of that today." Edwin paused to calculate.

"Henry Boll owned more land than that, of course. He bought and sold; started developments, that sort of thing."

"Made a fortune." Edwin shook his head in amazement.

"He lived well into his seventies; his wife, also. They had ten children. Your great-great-grandfather, who would also be my grandfather, was Jacob, the oldest."

"And Jacob built the rest of this house."

"Most of it. He was a doctor. I remember him. I was seven when he died. Very proper gentleman. Schooled in Europe."

"I guess Henry had the money to give his son the opportunity."

"My grandfather was named for his father's brother, Jacob Boll. He was an internationally known naturalist. Our most famous relative, I suppose."

They walked on through the music room.

"My grandparents added the front rooms there— the parlor, dining room, and then the kitchen and sunroom, and the gallery leading to the library. More bedrooms were added on the second floor. The original house upstairs is used for storage. Jacob had his office in the front parlor for many years."

She paused in the sunroom, and they looked out across the back garden.

"Henry's wife died first. Henry suffered ill health in his later years, and Jacob and his family moved back in to care for him. Your great grandfather Edward was Jacob's second oldest child. He was a tradesman."

"He had a mercantile store, I believe."

"Yes. Did quite well as Dallas grew. My father, Luis, was the youngest son. He and my mother lived here and took care of his parents in their last year. I was born here, in the front room upstairs."

"What business was your father in?"

"Railroads. He worked for the Houston Central at first, then became the director of several lines that met here in Dallas." Addy led on toward the library. "My father and mother added this room in 1924."

"I remember this from family Christmas celebrations when I was small." Edwin surveyed the room. "We always hung our stockings over there."

"Yes." Addy smiled remembering the big raucous celebrations. It was great fun for an only child with all the cousins around, then later all their children and grandchildren. Why had she stopped? Why had the family scattered so? She turned to look at her great nephew. He had been such a sweet child. Her favorite. Where had that little boy gone?

The two of them stood in the library for a while with their memories swirling around them.

"That's the house history basically. It has some romance to it, I think. Enough to warrant saving at any rate."

Edwin looked around at the rows of books. "I've been in this house hundreds of time, I guess, and I never realized the history. I was just a kid. I just took it all for granted." He smiled and shook his head. "So, now you have a chance to save it."

"I hope so."

"Yes, and I can see why. I suppose they have to document all the materials and additions and such."

"That's what Barton & Ramsey is doing now. In fact, you had said you wanted to meet Robyn."

"Yes, if possible. But I don't want to bother her."

"No, I told her you were coming." Adeline led the way toward the elevator. It was hard to keep a straight face. This was an Edwin she had not seen in many years. So polite, thoughtful. Whatever was he up to?

Robyn and Mary were hard at work going through file cabinets when Addy and Edwin got to the office. Robyn looked up when she heard their footsteps in the hall.

"Good afternoon." Addy called at the door. "May we interrupt for a moment?"

"Certainly." Robyn rose from her chair and waited for an introduction.

"Robyn, this my great nephew Edwin Bennett." She glanced back to Edwin. "Robyn Merrill."

They shook hands. "Nice to meet you at last, Robyn. I've been hearing quite a bit about you."

"Really?" Robyn motioned toward Mary. "This is my assistant, Mary Rennels."

Edwin nodded to the girl across the room. He took a deep breath and surveyed the room stacked with files. It smelled of musty paper and long undisturbed dust. "My, you do have your work cut out for you, I see."

Robyn laughed softly. "Yes, your ancestors were great savers, I think."

"Any progress?"

"Some." Robyn glanced at Addy, who was standing back observing Edwin with a curious look. "We have managed to determine the time period of some of the files. We are back to the turn of the century."

"What about the library addition plans," Addy asked.

"We found all the receipts carefully filed, but no architecture plans."

"You say you've determined which files go with which decade?" Edwin reached out to touch one of the file cabinets.

"Loosely," Robyn smiled. "Most of the records are carefully filed, but we find some things out of place once in a while. Mary found the car repair bills from 1918 with the household receipts from 1907. But that's a rare thing."

"I've always been a Civil War buff. Have you located that time period?"

"No, but you can see that we still have a lot to go through. Of course, those records would predate the 1880s house, they might not be stored here."

"What about the attic? Are there any papers stored up there? " Edwin looked around at Addy.

Adeline frowned slightly. "I don't know, Edwin. What makes you ask that?"

"Just curious. No particular reason." He looked back at Robyn. "How are you keeping this straight up here. There's so many cabinets."

"Stickers." Robyn held up a roll of yellow stickers. "When Mary or I finish one, we seal it shut with a couple of these."

"Very clever." Edwin took a step back. "Well, I don't want to take up any more of your time. We'll get out of your way." He placed a protective arm around Adeline's shoulders. "But you will let me know if you find the Civil War time period?"

"Sure, I'll do that."

"I'd love to look through it. Maybe I could come up here and sift through the files when you locate them." It was an open-ended remark that begged for a positive reply.

"We don't want to interrupt the girls." Adeline cautioned.

"No, certainly not." Edwin shook his head, but he still waited for Robyn's response.

"I'll let you know if we find the Civil War years." Robyn said, trying to avoid the invitation of Edwin's help.

Edwin and Adeline rode the elevator down without further comment. Edwin was preoccupied with his own thoughts it seemed, and Addy was still marveling at his newly-found pleasant personality.

"So" Edwin said, as they reached the first floor. "Anything else I should see today?"

"No. I guess that is about it."

They walked out the front door, and Edwin continued down the veranda to the far end with Addy following. "This old place was pretty well built to hold up this long, I guess."

Edwin tapped the trellis that closed off the end of the porch and shaded the area. He surveyed the veranda and then looked back at Addy. "Thanks for the tour. It will be interesting to see what all they find."

"Yes" Addy, head tilted back, studied him through the lower part of her glasses.

"I'm serious about the Civil War period though. Let me know if you find anything." He paused for a second. "In fact, I might just come over Saturday and look around myself."

Adeline started to object.

"Course, I'll be careful not to touch any of the files they have sealed."

"I don't think that's a very good idea. It will only add to the confusion up there. Let's just let Robyn work. She'll tell you if she finds anything."

Edwin looked as though he was ready to protest,

but then thought better of it. "I guess you're right. I'll check back with her … maybe tomorrow." He reached to give Adeline an uncharacteristic hug. "Thanks again." And he was gone.

Adeline watched him drive away before she went back in the house. She was totally dumbfounded with his behavior. This should be a good thing, having Edwin's support, right? So why did she feel so wary?"

Edwin glanced in his rearview mirror before he pulled out on Swiss Avenue. Addy was still standing on the porch. That had gone pretty well, he guessed. He hadn't found the records, but he had gotten a good look at the room and learned the girls' system. This was doable. And what could it hurt? His conscience tugged a little, but he wasn't actually doing anything that would physically harm Addy or the house. This was separate. It was Lancaster that Cavander was interested in, not this old house. And besides, he had to be practical. He had a family to consider.

Dallas 1865

By the light of a single lantern, Zebediah strained against the ropes as he lowered the crates one by one into the darkness. He worked quickly, sweat glistening on his brow, his breaths coming in rapid bursts as he lifted and shoved and guided the heavy loads. The boy might be out soon to milk and to offer his help, and this job was far from done. He hefted the last crate from the wagon and slid it after the others as morning light began to tint the horizon. Then without pause, he hurried down into the softening darkness and lifted the crates one by one over the half-built wall, stacking them in the narrow space.

When he finished, he covered them all quickly with the wagon sheet. At least now, if the boy came, there would be nothing to see.

That job accomplished, he paused to wipe his brow and straighten his back. Boss Henri could be at peace now. Zeb knew no one had seen them when they loaded the wagon in the yard. No one had seen him cross the Trinity just above Dowdy Ferry and guide the team up the trail around Dallas. Low clouds shielded the sliver of moon, and the ground muffled the wagon wheels in damp sand from an earlier shower. Now at the farmstead, he was shielded by trees, and buildings. No one had seen him pass.

And this place was safe. His repair of the foundation offered an answer. With most men gone to war, Zeb had found plenty of work doing odd labor for white folks. And at Boss Henri's insistence, the Tuckers had even let him keep his pay. Boss Henri had found him this job, for one of his old friends. He was good at stone work.

So when his boss told him about the guns, he knew just what to do. He was closing the wall today anyway. No one in the house would be the wiser. And he was glad to help his friend.

He placed the stones and mortar swiftly. No time to spare. The wall was shoulder high when he heard the boy.

"Good morning, Zebediah," he called down. "Do you need any help?"

"No," he called up. "I'm 'bout finished."

The gangly boy appeared in the opening, ducking under the low ceiling beams. "You got an early start today."

"I worked most all the night, I reckon. I got to get back and help Boss Henri this morning."

"Will the foundation be stronger now?"

"It will." Zebediah patted the stones by his shoulder. "You tell your mamma not to worry. The wall just needs to dry."

"I could help you clean up, if you need me."

"No, no, I'll be quick. You can go on with your chores. Don't worry your head about this."

The boy nodded and disappeared into the morning light.

Zebediah worked more slowly now, spreading the mortar and lifting the stones into place at the ceiling. He slid the last one in and stood back to survey his work, nodding in satisfaction.

Gathering his tools, he went out to the pump to wash them free of the remaining mortar, then splashing water over his head and neck, he shook the droplets from his beard. No turning back now. This was a powerful secret he carried. But it was a small task if he could repay Boss Henri's kindness.

CHAPTER 20

Dallas 2007

"I'm beginning to think our boy Bennett isn't going to come through on this," Cavander called to Murray Creed when he heard him enter the room. Cavander was bent over a large aerial photograph, studying it with a magnifying glass.

Creed closed the door behind him. "You might be right. We probably would have heard something immediately, if he had access to any papers."

"Well, we'll give him until Monday and see how resourceful he is." Cavander looked up and smiled. "Meanwhile, I have another idea. I got my pilot to take someone up and get an overall view of the property." The two men studied the photo.

"Interesting layout," Creed said.

"Yes, it's got real potential, I think. Good access to the freeway. Good location. We could build something nice out there … but take a closer look."

Creed leaned in.

"There's the house." Cavander pointed. "The drive. Then look just to the east. See that?" Cavander handed over the magnifying glass.

Creed took it and leaned down to study the area. "That's some sort of structure."

"Yes, it's a foundation. Must have been an old building there at one time, a shed or a barn maybe."

"Did Paul Henri mention a barn?"

"Not exactly. Just that he planned to store "the shipment," as he called it. He only mentioned that he would like to talk to Boll about getting the shipment out of Lancaster. Henry Boll was a close friend. His name keeps popping up everywhere else in the papers. It would be logical for Henri to confide in his friend, I'm guessing. And if the guns are with Boll, this might be the spot." He tapped the photograph. "The house was built much later. The shipment has to be somewhere in or around an older structure, if it's there at all."

They looked at the photo in silence for a while. "Could be it. I don't see much else around."

"I was checking the topography here." Cavander gestured at the map. "There is a line of trees across here between the house and this structure, and then the land seems to dip down some. See that?" He looked up at Creed. "I don't think you can see that foundation from the house. If it were a building, yes. But just the foundation … it's out of sight. Who do we know that could check this out for me?"

"Baxter would know about that, I think."

"Right." Cavander straightened. "Maybe a survey crew for a cable company, something like that as a cover."

"I'll get on it at once. Do you want him to excavate the site?"

"Not initially. Just survey, photographs, soil samples, like that."

"Right," Creed turned to go.

"Also, ask Baxter for a recommendation for some inside work."

Creed stopped halfway across the room and turned to study his boss with a worried look.

"If Bennett fails on this, we're going to need someone else to get a look at those records."

"That's risky."

Cavander looked up. "The risk is in waiting too long. Sooner or later someone else is going to stumble onto this."

"Right."

Cavander reached for a folder on his desk. Watching him, Creed paused longer and then asked, "Is there anything else?"

"Yes, maybe. I've got another idea. Something jumped out at me." He opened the folder. "I was reading over my notes on Paul Henri. I've got his records here. These Reunion people, they were strong against slavery. Right?"

"My understanding."

"One of these papers in here is a drawing of the Henri burial plot in Lancaster. It shows a map of the old graves and a copy of the gravestone inscriptions." Cavander smiled. "Someone did a good job of documenting all this for us, it seems. Henri and his wife and daughters were buried there together. He died in 1890. His daughters' husbands and children are also there, and then over to one side, is the grave of a slave." He paused to give Creed time to think about that. "Just the one grave. It says here the inscription read:

Zebediah
A Loyal Friend
Who Never Knew Freedom

"That's odd, don't you think? Paul Henri owning a slave?"

"When did he die?" Creed reached to take the map that Cavander offered. "Says here, March 1865."

"So during the war."

"Yes, one month before Lee surrendered." Cavander smiled. That would be bad luck, wouldn't it?"

"It would be unusual for a slave to be buried with his master, I think."

"Yes, I thought of that, too. Let's see what we can find out about this. See if there really is a slave buried there." He took the map back from Creed. "We may not need the Boll property at all. The guns might be right there under our noses."

"Any suggestions on where to find any information?"

Cavander considered the question for a moment. "Internet, maybe? County property rolls. They listed their slaves, I think. The graves are on public land. We'll have to get a permit to search.

"I'll look into it."

"Well, I talked to Penrow." Ramsey was saying as Robyn came into the conference room. A design team of six members was gathered around the table studying a map on the overhead. Robyn took a seat.

Ramsey continued, "They have several plans on the burner. None include the Boll property yet, so there's room to talk. Meanwhile, you can sort of see what they are thinking. Here's the hospital corridor, and that tapers down to apartments and condos. There on the northwest side there's light commercial, and Vander Corporation has recently acquired the land on the south side. Plug in some high rise upscale buildings over here, and what do you begin to see?"

"They could be thinking shopping center." "Yes, but what's another possibility?"

"A nice big green area on the Boll property." one of the group said.

Ramsey nodded. "There's a small collection of 1800s houses clustered near her house, just across Swiss Avenue there. We want to preserve them also, if possible. So put on your thinking caps."

"Pioneer village?" someone suggested.

"We already have one of those at Old City Park." They studied the map in silence.

"That's our problem," Ramsey said after a bit. "We need some fresh ideas. Keep thinking. In the meantime our firm can develop designs for any number of the buildings along here. I have a list of companies. We'll split these up and get started on proposals. Anything else?"

. "One thing I thought of last night was the eco system on the Boll property. If we're thinking park land, what would we be preserving?"

"Good point, Ted. You're our landscape specialist. What do you think?"

"We need a survey of plant life, elevation map, and an on-site study."

"Work that up and get back to me."

The design team members made hasty notes as the conversation flowed back and forth across the table.

By noon a skeleton plan was in place, and the meeting broke up.

Robyn left the room on a high. It was great to see a design team in action. She grabbed a sandwich at the deli and headed for the Boll Mansion.

"Well, I've found the 1800s," Mary said as Robyn walked in.

"Really! What have you got?"

"Nothing too exciting yet, but we're in the right century.

Robyn looked over Mary's shoulder. "1889, very good."

"I've got more receipts. Something about some dining chairs. A Mr. Louis Van Gronderbeck built eight chairs for Jacob Boll."

"Addy said the chairs were made by one of the colonists. She still has three of them downstairs. Beautiful carvings."

"There's a final receipt for the house construction here too. No particulars about the materials, but apparently Boll paid someone named Charles Capy five thousand dollars for the house. That can't be right."

"Probably it is. Five thousand would get you a pretty fancy place in 1889."

"Amazing."

"Hand me some of those files. This looks promising."

They worked the rest of the afternoon and the rest of the week. But still no specific design plans turned up.

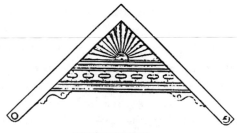

CHAPTER 21

Edwin Bennett could not believe he was doing this. Could not believe it! He felt like an idiot. All dressed out in black like some B-rated ninja movie. But it didn't stop him. It had been over a week, and he had not heard a word from that girl about the Civil War papers. His time was running out. Cavander wasn't going to wait forever. So here he was about to add breaking and entering to his list of transgressions.

He parked across the street, checked both directions, and climbed out of his car. He carried a small black zippered bag containing wire cutters, masking tape, a pry bar, and a flashlight. He pulled on his gloves. Okay, get this over with!

The traffic was almost nonexistent at this hour. At 3:00 A.M., everyone with any sense was at home, he thought as he crossed the street and slipped through the driveway entry.

Careful to stay on the grass and off the gravel, he

crossed the lawn in a scurrying crouch. He could just make out the columns on the veranda, and above that the framed windows on the second floor. This would be the tricky part, but if he could climb the trellis at the end of the porch, he would be on the roof in no time.

He slipped the strap of his bag over his shoulder and tested the first rung of the wooden lattice work. Pretty sturdy. He scrambled up, oblivious to the rose thorns snagging at his clothing and scratching his face. The roof ledge was a challenge. He grasped desperately in the dark for any hold he could feel on the roof. There was a moment just as he reached the top where he thought he was falling backward, but he flattened himself against the shingles and found his balance. The slope of the veranda roof was slight, so he belly crawled up to the window ledge and pushed at the sash. No good. But it wasn't locked. Please don't let it be locked. He carefully took his pry bar out of his bag and inserted it. The window slid up with only a slight creak. So far so good.

Inside the room, he crouched down and flipped on his light. It was a military style that mounted on his shoulder so his hands would be free. He smiled at his cleverness. Who knew there was an actual spy store in Dallas where you could get such things. He had found the store in the yellow pages—Spy Wares, or something like that.

Now, he cautioned himself, don't move anything. He directed his light to various file cabinets sporting the bright yellow stickers. The girls had even dated them. Good job. In the far corner of the room set a double stack of cabinets yet unmarked. That would be his target.

Edwin eased across the room as silently as he could. No sound would be best. He felt sure Addy would not hear him from the other side of the house, and the housekeeper's room was behind the kitchen on the first floor. If he could just manage not to drop anything heavy, he was safe.

He started at one end of the cabinets, sliding the drawer out slowly. The first one was stuffed with papers. He would do a quick scan of all the drawers looking for anything that looked like a journal. Cavander had seemed most interested in Henry Boll's personal papers. That might cut down on his search time.

But nothing turned up. Two hours later he still had nothing. He had not even been able to establish dates on most of the files. He glanced out the window to see a slight softening of the darkness. He had to clear out of here before it got any lighter. Damn it! This little exercise would have to be finished another night. He checked to see that all looked undisturbed and retraced his steps to the window and down the trellis. He had just enough time to get home and change before Marla woke up. He would just say he fell asleep in his study. She would believe that.

Wednesday night was no better. He got started a little earlier, around 2:00, by telling Marla he was working late at the office and would just sleep on his sofa there. That gave him another hour, but he still came up empty. And the best part was, it was misting rain when he left at 5:00. Perfect!

On Thursday Murray Creed called to check on his progress. Edwin had to confess no results, but he assured him he was working on it.

"Good ... Say Edwin, what's the layout over there?"

"Layout?"

"Any out-buildings, like barns, storage sheds, things like that from the right period of time?"

"No. I don't believe so. I think everything has been

torn down over the years. Why do you ask?"

"Just curious. Something he turned up in his research. Talk to you soon." And the line went dead.

Edwin stared at the phone in his hand. Out- buildings? What the hell … ? What was Cavander looking for? Here he was scrambling around like a cat burglar, and he had no idea what he was looking for. Cavander had led him to believe he was searching for something to do with his property in Lancaster, but now he wants to know about something at Addy's house? This doesn't sound right.

He clicked on his laptop and went to the Internet. Let's see. Where to start. Google Henry Boll and see what happens. The machine whirred and a site popped up. Wow! Henry Boll. He had an entry. Who would have thought it? He scanned down the page.

Henry Boll 1830—1904 … Canton Aargan, Switzerland.

The son of … educated in Zurich … apprentice to a large meat processing plant …

Had the misfortune of losing his wife and both children …

Became interested in a colony being organized for Texas …

1855 married Elizabeth Knapfli … also a colonist.

Enlisted in Confederate army in 1862 … Commissary Department in Waco, Texas … in charge of military food and provisions …

Following the Civil War served as city and county treasurer in 1869 for Dallas … prominent citizen …

Not much there. Try Henri.

Paul Henri —1890 … born in Charletretreau, France … married Adelaide Dehouge. Educated in some of the best schools in France … became an engraver and designer.

Became interested in the European American Society of Colonization ... 1855 made trip to Dallas ... helped to prepare fields for production of food.

1863 joined the Confederate Army and was assigned to Tucker & Sharrard arms factory in Lancaster, Texas ...

After the war entered into the mercantile business in Lancaster ... civic leader ...

Well, there is the Lancaster connection. Is Cavander looking for something to do with the arms factory? Is he a collector? Tucker & Sharrard? Okay, try that. He typed in the words and got a new screen.

No matches found for Tucker & Sharrard.

He stared at the notation. No matches? Great! He spent the next half hour entering anything he could think of that related to the Civil War and came up hopelessly lost in a stream of useless entries. Cavander is nuts! This is hopeless. He had better things to do than this.

With as little sleep as he was getting, he was accomplishing very little on the job. If he could just put his head down for a few minutes ... not a good idea.

He had an email from Weldon Shanks, his message bar announced. Great! Shanks probably had heard about Barton & Ramsey helping Adeline research the house. He didn't open the message. The longer he could avoid Shanks on this, the better.

He made some excuse about an appointment and skipped out a side door. He felt as if his whole world was caving in on him. The house search business was actually helping by keeping him occupied. He couldn't deal with Shanks just yet. Whether Cavander was crazy or not, the job offer was nothing to ignore. He would live up to his part of the bargain. With Cavander behind him, Shanks would have to give him the consultant assignment. No one disagreed with Mitchell Cavander. Vander Corporation was one of the firm's largest accounts. He would give his search one more chance.

But it rained. Not just a shower this time. A deluge! At 3:00 in the morning Edwin admitted defeat. He couldn't go back in that house without leaving an obvious trail of water and mud. He went home and gratefully crawled into bed.

CHAPTER 22

Robyn reported her findings every week just to keep Ramsey up to date. There had not been much to discuss so far, but the 1880 papers were interesting. "Along with the receipt for the house construction, there was a copy of the work order for brick to build the foundation. They used a company called Frichot Brothers. I looked it up on line, and Hershel and Pere Philip Frichot were also La Reunion colonists."

"Yes, like I said the other day, brick making and cement were two of the very first industries in Dallas. And both types of companies were started by La Reunion people."

Ted Wilson, the landscape specialist, stuck his head in the door. "Hi. Got a minute?"

"Sure thing."

"I've been working on the physical survey of the Boll acreage. This morning I walked over the property with the survey team to get an overview, and we ran on to something I think you need to know about." He placed several 8x10 photos on the table. "Someone's been out there recently."

Ramsey studied the first photo and then handed it to Robyn. "Who do you think it is?"

No idea. But it looks like they were using survey equipment and taking soil samples. As you can see they did some digging next to this old foundation."

"Did Adeline mention that anyone had contacted her?"

"No, or Gladys either." Robyn said.

"There were a couple of marker flags with Ace Cable on them laying on the ground like they had been dropped, but I checked it out, and there is no such company listed in the Metroplex."

"What is that structure?"

"By the size of it, I would guess an old barn or some kind of shed."

"Adeline said there had been a garage, and she had it torn down several years ago." Robyn offered.

"How could someone be out there, and no one in the house know it?"

"There's no gate. And there's a line of trees between this spot and the house. I guess anyone could come in if they were determined," Ted said.

"I think we need to let Adeline know about this and then possibly the police, if she has no idea. Meanwhile, what have you found out about the land?"

"Well, there's some good stands of native trees out there. Most of the land was used for grazing, I think, so it's pretty undisturbed. I've got people working on that. There's a stream bed, but not much water. There's good possibilities for open use areas."

"Good. When do you think you'll have your report?"

"Couple of weeks."

"Let me know if you see anything else unusual out there. I'll follow up on this."

Adeline and Gladys were as surprised as everyone else about the intruder. Robyn walked out to the old foundation with them after she told them about the discovery.

Whoever it was had dug several deep holes next to the old foundation, apparently with an auger, as if they were taking samples of some sort. The ground was fairly muddy from the last rain, but there were only faint tracks, Robyn noticed. Whoever did this was out here several days ago before the rain.

"Was there a basement to this building?

"I believe so. I think they stored tools down there." Adeline placed her hand on the tallest part of the foundation for support. "I never saw it as a barn. It was a garage for as long as I remember. My father converted it when he bought a car. There were some rooms up top for the gardener. When I had it torn down the workmen filled the lower part for safety's sake."

"We need to call the police on this. This is trespassing." Gladys said.

"I suppose you're right." Adeline said. "I'll go back to the house and call."

A patrol car showed up first. Robyn listened as Adeline and Gladys gave the officer their information. Then, as they walked out to the old foundation, another car arrived. These men were in street clothes.

Apparently a disturbance at the Boll Mansion warranted detectives, Robyn thought. She excused herself and went back to her research. There was nothing she could add to the discussion.

After about thirty minutes, she heard the elevator and then voices in the hall. Adeline appeared at the door, and two men were with her. "Robyn, these men are police detectives. I was telling them that you were working up here, and they wanted to meet you."

"Certainly."

"Warren Evans," the older man said, "and this is my partner, Noah Garrison." The younger man nodded and stepped forward to shake her hand. He had the clearest blue eyes she had ever seen.

"Pardon the interruption, but we wanted to confirm that you hadn't observed anything unusual that might help us out."

"No problem. I would be glad to help out if I could, but I haven't noticed anything."

"You are with Barton & Ramsey, I understand," the younger of the two detectives said.

"Yes."

"Looks like you have a lot of material to go through up here. Are you working alone?"

"No, I have an assistant. She's just not here today."

"Mind if we look around?"

"Go right ahead, if you can. It's rather crowded in here. We haven't tried to get over to the back of the room yet."

The two men worked their way carefully through the tables and cabinets. "You say you haven't been over here?" The older man asked.

"No, we are working our way across. We'll tackle those cabinets when we finish with these closer ones."

The older detective motioned to the second man,

who moved closer, and they both stared down at the floor. "Someone's been over here," the younger man said. "There are tracks everywhere in the dust." They moved toward the window carefully avoiding stepping on the tracks. "Let's get a team up here. Someone's been through this window."

"Right."

Robyn and Adeline watched in stunned silence. "Please stay out of this area until we can get someone up here to check these prints."

The two women nodded dumbly and then looked at one another.

"I'll check outside." The older man left the room. The younger man pulled out a notebook. "I'll need the name of your assistant."

"Mary Rennels. She's a student intern with Barton & Ramsey. She's at the office now. I could call her."

"If you don't mind."

The first man appeared at the door again. "You need to see this." The two detectives left.

"Well, I never!" Adeline said.

CHAPTER 23

The upshot of it all was that Robyn got no more research done that afternoon. The room was swarming with police within the hour, taking photographs and dusting for prints. Mary came after Robyn called her and gave a statement. The police had more questions for Robyn as well, and the one with the blue eyes was particularly thorough.

"You're an architect with Barton & Ramsey?"

"Yes. We're researching this house for possible historic designation."

"Have you been with the firm long?"

"No. I've recently joined."

"Where were you employed prior to that?"

Robyn hesitated. Surely he didn't think she had anything to do with this. "Atlanta," she answered after a moment.

"Well, welcome to Texas," he said with a crooked smile that took her by surprise. The smile vanished and his professional voice took over again. "Can you think of anyone who might be interested enough in your work to break in up here?"

"No, I'm sorry. I'm totally surprised by this," she answered, but her thoughts weren't on the question. They were on the smile he had just given her.

"If you think of anything, anything at all, would you give me a call? He handed her a card. "My number is on there."

"Certainly."

"Now, if I could get your full name and address, phone number, and so on, I think that will be it."

"Robyn Merrill"

"Mrs. or Miss?"

"Ms." He had his head down writing, but she could swear she caught a bit of that crooked little smile again. "5700 Blackburn." She added her apartment number and cell phone.

"Great." The detective looked up. Thank you, Ms. Merrill. Again, I'm Noah Garrison. I'll be in touch, I'm sure." And he was gone.

Robyn watched him disappear out the door and then glanced at Mary, who was studying her from her desk.

"He's so cute!" Mary mouthed silently.

Robyn shot her a horrified look and turned away.

With all the excitement, the girls decided to call it a day. They stood little chance of getting any work done anyway. Robyn stopped by to check on Gladys and Adeline on her way out. She found Gladys in the kitchen.

"Adeline is lying down. It's been a troubling day,"

Gladys said as Robyn walked in.

"To say the least. Did the police tell you anything?"

"No, just asked a lot of questions." Gladys folded and smoothed a cup towel she was holding. "I bet Edwin had something to do with this."

Robyn blinked. "I hadn't thought of him. Surely not, Gladys. He seemed so nice the other day."

"Humph!" Gladys turned her back and closed a drawer with more force than necessary.

"He's Adeline's closest relative. Why would he break in? He could get any information he needed from Adeline, couldn't he?"

Gladys seemed to waver a little. "I just don't trust him, that's all. He might have been nice the other day, but you should have heard him a few weeks ago. I don't trust him."

"Well, let's not upset Adeline any more with this. Let the police do their job." She waited for a response from Gladys, but none came. "You need to get some rest too, I think. I'll see you tomorrow."

When she went out to her car, the police were still at the old barn site. She saw the detective talking with an officer. What was his name? Noah something. And Mary was right. He was a very handsome man.

The men were putting up barrier tape around the old foundation. Well, these people are nothing if not thorough, she thought as she left.

⟳⟲

By the next morning, Adeline was rested and ready to look at this new development with a clear eye. Someone, reasons unknown, had broken into her home while she and Gladys slept, presumably. She thought back over the last week or so. She could remember no incident, no noise that had drawn her attention. The idea of being helpless while someone prowled through her house should have terrified her, she knew, but her first reaction instead was one of astonishment. How could someone do this? And why?

When she went down to breakfast, she expected a reaction from Gladys since she wasn't much for disruption around the house. But Gladys didn't even mention the break-in. She just met her with a smile and cup of coffee. Her only comment was, "Do you think those people are all finished?"

"Yes, I think so. I can't imagine what else they could need."

"I was thinking of going down to the City Market today. Maybe find some produce to put up."

"Yes, that would be nice. I might go with you." Then Adeline settled in behind the morning paper, and Gladys set the kitchen right.

In the Metro section of the paper, the break-in was mentioned in a small article.

> Police were called to investigate a possible break-in and trespassing incident at a historic home on Swiss Avenue.

But the thing that caught her attention was the final sentence.

> The property is part of an area destined for development. Several major companies are reported to be involved in proposals for future projects.

Adeline frowned and read the statement a second time. It sounded so definite, and she had agreed to nothing. She crushed the paper in her haste to close it. Gladys looked around to see what the commotion was.

155

"This whole thing is getting out of hand," Adeline said.

Gladys shrugged her shoulders. "Did you expect anything else?"

Adeline frowned again. Trust Gladys to pin her down with one of her dry comments. "Well, I'm calling Grayson." She stood up and steadied herself for a second, and then marched out of the room. Luckily, she couldn't see the smile on Gladys' face.

CHAPTER 24

It was the next day before Adeline thought of calling Edwin to tell him about the break-in. Even then she almost didn't. She could just imagine his reaction. All fuss and feathers about how dangerous it was for her to stay in the house. Just another excuse for him to try to pressure her into moving. But then she knew he would have to find out eventually, and it was best he hear it from her.

However, Edwin's reaction surprised her. He seemed dumbstruck at first, more interested in how she had discovered the intruder than anything else. He actually didn't admonish her for placing herself in danger at all. He just asked what the police had found.

"Nothing out of place that I know of," Adeline said. "But they certainly seem thorough, with all their photos and dusting and measuring,"

"And nothing is missing?"

"No, it appears they never tried to enter the rest of

the house. Just came in the one window and ..."

"So the police found nothing?"

"Well, some footprints, I think ..."

"Footprints? Where? Could they identify them?"

"I have no idea, Edwin. They haven't confided in me."

"And you say whoever it was, also was digging out at the old garage?"

"Yes, making deep holes. I'm just completely amazed. Whatever could it be they were hunting?"

"There's just no telling, Addy. Just no way to know, I guess. Please keep me posted on this."

"You might want to come over when the detectives report their findings."

"No, no, I don't need to butt in. What could I possibly add? Just let me know what they find."

"I will."

Edwin dropped the phone in the cradle and slumped back in his chair. Holy Mother ... what have I done? Did I touch anything? Leave any prints? No, no, I was wearing gloves. But my shoes? Could they trace those? They can find you by the tread pattern, can't they? It was on that crime show. I've got to get rid of those shoes! His mind was racing, and he was suddenly sweating as though he had been running.

Wait, wait now; don't panic. There is nothing to tie me to the scene. Nothing. Thank God I didn't go back over there. In all that mud I would have left plenty of tracks. Then the thought struck him that maybe he did anyway! He mopped at his forehead with his handkerchief. But it had rained, remember? The rain would have washed any prints. Just get hold of yourself!

His telephone signaled an incoming call. He stared at the blinking light. Not now! He was too flustered to talk to anyone. He sat stone still staring at the light and tried to calm his breathing and heart rate.

And the trespassing part, he thought suddenly. Who could that be? He had been so rattled by the break-in discovery, he had ignored the rest. Who would do that? And Cavander flashed in his mind. Creed had asked about old buildings on the grounds. Could it be Cavander?

What a mess! He should have never gone over there, never listened to Cavander. If this got out, he was ruined! He needed time to think.

So, assume Cavander ordered the digging. Why? What could possibly be that important? Cavander was no different than him. If he got caught up in this some way, it would ruin him, too.

He pulled a small flask of vodka from his second desk drawer and took a swallow. He had to think clearly now. Just slow down.

The phone light flashed again. He hesitated, then pressed the button to take the call.

"You're a hard man to get hold of," Murray Creed said in an icy tone.

"I've been busy." Edwin cleared his throat.

"Does that mean you have something to report?"

"Yes, it does. There's been someone out at the house. The police were called."

He was answered by silence on the line. "And how would this concern me?" Creed responded after a few seconds.

"I have no idea. I'm just telling you. I can't check on anything."

"So you have no information for me?"

"I'm working on it."

"See that you are. We'll give you a little more time." And the line went dead.

Murray Creed hung up the phone and stared at it for several seconds as though it were a live creature that he expected to move. 'The police were called' was ringing in his ears. Damn Baxter! How could he slip up like this? He's a professional. Damage control. What was his next step? Alert Baxter. Make sure he had covered all his movements. Update Cavander. Not a pleasant thought. How the hell could this happen?

He dialed Baxter's number and heard his deep monotone voice.

"There's been an incident."

No response.

"Our last contract. It has been compromised. Is there any … ?"

"All taken care of."

"The truck?"

"I had to replace the tires. Normal procedure."

"And that is done?"

"Affirmative."

"Any chance of … ?"

"Personnel all accounted for. No problem."

"You're sure."

"Yes."

"Who has the materials?"

"Your lab."

"So we are all clear?"

"Yes, no problem."

Creed clicked the phone off and took a deep breath. At least he had something positive to report. He headed for Cavander's office.

"How could they find it so quickly?" was Cavander's first question.

He actually took the news fairly well, considering. Maybe because he only had himself to blame, Creed thought. He had cautioned against the idea, but Cavander had insisted.

'Well, we're clear. We'll just wait this out. Bennett has no idea we are involved. Right?"

"There's no reason for him to suspect."

"Hmmm," Cavander twirled a letter opener shaped like a samurai sword between his fingers. "So ... , we wait to hear this from the outside. No reason to react. No harm done."

Creed nodded and turned to go.

"What else did Bennett have to say? Anything?"

"He said he was working on it."

Cavander nodded. "We'll give him a little more time."

"Right."

"How are you coming on the slave information?"

"Nothing yet."

"And Baxter. What did he find out there?"

"Everything is at the lab."

"Keep me posted."

As the hours went by, Edwin's thoughts became clearer. This changed everything. No agreement with Cavander, no partnership was worth this. He had to look out for himself. If this caved in on Cavander and Creed, he knew they would pull him under immediately. He had to act first. But how?

First of all, he needed to know what it was Cavander was chasing. It had to be valuable if he were willing to risk all this, to enlist his help, plus go snooping on his own.

He clicked on his computer again. Maybe he missed something before.

This time he entered **Lancaster, Texas Tucker & Sharrard.**

The computer whirred and a screen popped up. **No entry found. Do you mean Tucker & Sherrard?** He stared at the question. Could it really be that simple? Just a spelling error? He retyped his request and instantly a new screen appeared.

Tucker & Sherrard

Very rare Tucker & Sherrard 1st Dragoon Revolver ... produced in Lancaster, Texas, .44 caliber copy of the Colt Dragoon Model.

Argyle William Tucker and his parents moved to Texas in 1854 ... began making guns in 1856 on the frontier.

Military Board of Texas contacted the Tuckers during the Civil War ... created the Tucker & Sherrard .44-caliber pistol.

Tucker Sherrard & Company of Lancaster, Dallas County, Texas. Their contract ... 3,000 pistols.

Supplies were hard to come by ... shop continued to make firearms as the war was coming to an end ...

There was a picture of the Tucker & Sherrard pistol and several other sites to check. He clicked on another one.

Only four Tucker & Sherrard pistols known to be in existence today.
No clear record that contract was fulfilled.

He clicked back to his first entry and read further down.

It was apparent the South was losing and the Tuckers, who usually only accepted gold for their services anyway, decided to turn away Confederate money and require payment in gold.
Tucker fell under suspicion of treason ... factory was left under control of Paul Henri, an engraver and employee.

There was his man. Edwin stared at the screen. Gold? What was the value of 3,000 guns in 1864? How much gold are we talking about? He quickly scribbled on a note pad. Say the 3,000 guns cost $40 dollars each. That's $120,000. How much gold was that? What was the value of gold in 1864?

He clicked back to the home page and typed in his question. The screen popped up after a few seconds. Between $165 and $179 per ounce in the Civil War years. Let's say $179. He scribbled on his pad again. Let's see. $179 divided into $120,000: that's 670 ounces. What's gold worth right now? What did the paper say? $1,200 an ounce? 670 times 1,200 equals

$804,000! Is that what Cavander is looking for? He clicked back to the site for the guns.

The mystery of the Lancaster gun factory has never been explained. Some records show only 1,000 guns were ever shipped out. Only four guns are known to exist today, and although the gold shipment was authorized, it has never been accounted for.

Edwin sat back and stared at the screen. So something Cavander found in Paul Henri's papers has him thinking that the guns, or the gold, or both, are buried on the Boll property. Eight hundred thousand dollars in gold and maybe 2,000 guns missing. And who knows what the guns might be worth to collectors? Enough for Mitchell Cavander to take some risks. Especially if he had a sucker like me to sacrifice, if his plans fell through.

Edwin clicked off his computer and stared at the blank screen. He had to plan.

CHAPTER 25

Robyn and Mary got back to work two days later. The crime lab people were finished working in their room, so things settled back into routine. They were almost finished with the first set of file cabinets and would be ready to tackle the double stacked set along the far wall; the ones that had attracted so much attention. So far the pertinent information they had found on the house was minimal. Rather discouraging really, but it had to be here. Robyn just kept clinging to the belief that as meticulous as Adeline's ancestors had been with all the minutia of sales receipts and cancelled checks, they had to have valued the house plans. But their first day back yielded nothing new.

Mary left a little early to meet an appointment, and Robyn stopped off downstairs to say goodbye to Adeline. She heard voices from the sunroom and headed that way expecting to see Gladys and Adeline. But it was the younger detective who was sitting at the table with Addy.

"Oh, I'm sorry. I didn't mean to interrupt."

The detective stood when he saw her.

"Yes, how are you?"

"Noah," he said with that crooked smile of his. "You can both just call me Noah."

Adeline motioned for Robyn to join them at the table.

Robyn followed Addy's instructions and then looked at the detective. "So, are you here to report that our mystery is solved?"

"No, not today. I just wanted to bring Mrs. Sinclair up to date. We don't have much to go on, I'm afraid. As far as we can tell, other than a little dirt at the garage site, nothing is missing."

"Still, breaking in, that's serious." Robyn said. "I mean, what if they come back?"

"Exactly. That's why we are trying to cover all the possibilities. Why the case is still open."

"Well, I appreciate your effort," Adeline said. "And I'm sure Robyn does, also."

Robyn caught the sting of a reprimand in Addy's voice. Was she coming across as rude? "Yes, of course. And it was good to get back to work." She looked at Adeline. "We finished the front files today. We'll be starting on the other set tomorrow."

"I'm sorry this has been such an ordeal. I hope it hasn't all been in vain."

"No, I can't believe that. We'll find the plans, I'm sure. Meanwhile ..." She glanced back at the detective. "I'll leave you two to your conference. I need to stop back by the office."

Noah rose as she did. "I was just about to leave myself. I'll walk you to your car." He looked back at Adeline. "Unless you have more questions."

"No, just thank you for coming."

They said their good byes to Adeline who smiled as though she was in on some secret, Robyn thought.

"I'm sorry I interrupted your meeting." Robyn said as they went down the front steps.

"No problem. I was finished. I was just enjoying talking to Mrs. Sinclair."

"She is a delight, isn't she?"

He reached to open her car door for her. "So, just how serious are you about going back to your office? Could I talk you into a drink instead?'

"A drink? Aren't you on duty?"

Noah glanced at his watch. "Not as of fifteen minutes ago. Coffee, tea, margarita, beer ... whatever." There was that smile again.

Noah waited a moment as if he hoped she would change her mind. "Well, another time, maybe."

Robyn smiled. "Thank you for understanding." She fumbled with her ignition key and backed around straight in the drive way while he stood watching.

He was still there when she glanced in the side mirror as she turned on to Swiss Avenue. Her heart was pounding as though she had been running, escaping actually. Gracious! He had just asked her out. No, she wasn't ready for that. She just wasn't ready.

Adeline smiled to herself as the two young people left. Obviously, the young detective had other reasons to drop by besides updating her. He had certainly jumped at the chance to talk to Robyn. Good. They would make a nice couple, and she worried about Robyn not getting out more. She just seemed to work around the clock.

She heard the phone in the front hall, but she knew Gladys would answer. Then she heard her footsteps across the kitchen before Gladys appeared at the door.

"That was Mr. Chandler. He asked if you were busy and could he come over for a visit. I told him fine. He'll be here shortly."

"Did he say what he wanted?"

"Just to talk to you. Something about the house probably."

"Yes," Adeline said, but with no conviction. It was her special request. And if a phone message couldn't cover it …

It was a short drive from Grayson's office, and he knocked at the door, it seemed, in only minutes. Gladys showed him into the sunroom.

"Hello, Adeline. How are you today?"

"Very well, and you?"

"Can't complain. Busy and that's a good thing." Grayson fell silent.

"I believe you must have something to tell me if you took time to drive over."

"Yes, I do. … I don't know quite how to begin except to remind you that you wanted complete truth."

"Yes."

"I had one of my clerks do some checking on the name you gave me." Grayson eased into a chair across from Adeline. "It was there in the paper, February

7th, just as Harriet said." He cleared his throat. "The woman had been living in a nursing home down there for the last five years. Apparently, she had no family, no children. I took up the investigation from there to keep it just between you and me."

Adeline nodded her appreciation.

"The woman had been a housemaid down there for many years. All her life, actually. Worked for several different families. Her given name was Etta Sinclair. I made a trip down there this last Monday. The nursing home said they still had her personal effects waiting for someone to claim them. Since I was interested, they were all too happy to turn them over to me."

Grayson took a long deep breath. "She didn't have much—some clothing which I left there as a donation, and a few personal things. Trinkets that probably had special meaning for her. The one thing of real interest was this."

He laid a large envelope on the table. "It's a picture of her and her husband—a wedding picture." He pulled it out of the envelope and handed it to Adeline.

It was Albert. A younger man, but all the same. it was him.

"There's a note on the back there."

Adeline turned the picture over. It was a date, probably a wedding date.

May 14, 1932
Albert & Etta Sinclair

Adeline felt as if all the air had left her body. She sat frozen staring at the date. 1932. Five years before she met Albert. Six before they married.

"I checked the records at the courthouse. There was a marriage certificate, but no record of a divorce. The

169

people at the nursing home told me that her bills were covered by a trust. I checked with the executor, and he told me it had been set up in 1942 by Mr. Sinclair to provide income for her. The name, social security number, everything matched your Albert."

They sat in silence for a time.

"I'm sorry, Adeline." Grayson said after a bit. "I wish I didn't have to tell you this. It serves no purpose after all these years, but I promised you the truth and …"

"No," Addy's voice was only a whisper. "No, you were right to tell me. Thank you for your honesty."

"Is there anything I can do for you now? Should I call Gladys?"

"No, I'm fine. I'll be fine." She reached to squeeze his outstretched hand. "You can go now. I'll be fine."

Grayson left quietly. Addy heard the front door close and the muffled engine of his car. She rose slowly and went to the parlor to look at Albert's portrait over the fireplace. He looked so successful in that pose. She had looked at the portrait for over sixty years and imagined what their life would have been if he had survived the war. The years they would have had together. And all the time … all that time, he had had another life, another wife.

She suddenly felt very weak. She sat down on the sofa. Why Albert? Why?

But she knew why. Down deep, she knew. Her father was wealthy and very persuasive. She had been a prize catch back then. To a poor man, the opportunity would have been hard to resist.

She sat for a long time looking at the painting, replaying their short life together in her mind like a movie reel. Strangely, she thought, there were no tears. Such a shock. Such betrayal, and yet she had no tears. Light began to fade into evening, and the room grew darker.

"Oh, here you are." Gladys called from the door way. I thought you had gone upstairs. Are you feeling all right?"

"Yes, I'm fine. What time is it?"

"A little past seven. Are you hungry? I have some supper fixed."

"Yes, thank you." Adeline rose and carefully steadied her balance. "Supper would be nice."

CHAPTER 26

Creed took the lab report to Cavander as soon as he got it. Mitchell Cavander had been in conference with visiting industrialists from Indonesia for the last three days. Creed knew information on his boss's latest diversion would be welcome. Cavander was like a kid with his baseball cards when it came to his weapons collection.

Cavender pushed aside the thick report he was reading and took the envelope immediately. "What have you found out about the grave in Lancaster?"

"Working on it. Nothing yet."

"What about Bennett? Have you heard from him?" He said, as he opened the lab report.

"No, I was thinking of calling today."

"Well, let's see what this says first." Cavander studied the paper and frowned. "Not much here." He handed it to Creed, who scanned down the first page.

"Fifty by seventy-five feet. By the size of the foundation, I would say it was definitely a barn at one time." He flipped to the second page. "And the soil sample shows nothing, just rubble and dirt. Probably fill when the building was taken down just to cover the basement cavity."

Cavander took the report back and looked at it again. "Says here the upper soil was loose down to seven feet, then hard packed. That must be the original base."

"Something could be buried below that, and no one would be the wiser."

"Right." Cavender studied the sheet. "Problem is, now they'll be watching the area since the police were called. We can't pursue this."

Creed let out a silent breath of relief. He had been worried that Cavander would not give up. He could be very myopic when he was on a quest.

The two men stared at the report in silence. "How are they funding the research and restoration over there?" Cavander asked, to himself as much as to Creed.

"No idea. Barton & Ramsey is doing it at this point, I suppose. They may be trying to enlist one of the historical society groups."

"How about we volunteer? They probably would welcome some financial help, and we could start with the old barn while they are still stalled on the house."

"It could work."

"Community cooperation, that sort of thing. It could improve our chances on winning the land bid, also."

"I'll get in touch with Dalton Ramsey and try to work something out."

The two men smiled. It was great when a new plan jelled.

"And stay on the slave thing out in Lancaster."

"Right."

Mary found the records for the 1860s in the second file cabinet in the bottom row. The files were so fragile Robyn was afraid to go through them. It took days to place each paper in a plastic sleeve where it could be handled safely. And most of the items were the usual—receipts, bills, payment stubs, lists of expenses. However, they could leave nothing to chance. There might be something.

And there was. Buried in a stack of accounting sheets was a handwritten receipt showing that thirty-four dollars was paid for materials to shore up a foundation wall in March 1865. That would have to be some building at the old farmstead. This was their first bit of information on the original buildings. After all their search, Robyn and Mary felt as though they had discovered a gold mine of information. It was cause for celebration.

As they hurried back to the office, they stopped by to tell Addy about their find.

"My great-grandfather was away at war in 1865, I believe. He was assigned to the Confederate supply depot in Waco during those years. I suppose he or his wife hired someone to do this work for him while he was away."

"What foundation do you think it means? Robyn asked. "The house, the barn, or something else?" They all thought about that for a minute.

"Well, it sounds very promising anyway." Addy said.

"Yes, finally!" Robyn laughed. "Listen, Mary and I are going to run get some lunch and check in at the office. We'll be back around 3:00."

Ramsey was pleased at their news. He had the office staff proceeding on the application for historic designation. They had collected most of the needed interviews and information, and were just waiting on the house records.

"I got an interesting call from Mitchell Cavander this morning. At least it was his right hand man, Murray Creed. He's offering to fund our research at the Boll Mansion and handle some of the heavy work. He proposed doing the excavation work and restoration of any outbuildings."

"What do you think about that?" Robyn asked.

"Well, it would be good to get some financial backing."

"Why would Cavander be interested in this?"

"Good question. My guess is he's looking for some edge to improve his chances on the land sale. There are three companies bidding on it: Vander, Penrow, and Andover-Warren."

"So what did you tell him?"

"I said it wasn't my decision to make. That I would relay his proposal to Adeline and her lawyer. Probably they are going to be reluctant to grant any favors while bids are still being considered."

"Interesting ... Well, Mary and I just dropped by to check in and report our find. We're on our way back to the house."

CHAPTER 27

"That nice young detective called," Adeline said. She and Robyn were enjoying some of Gladys' pound cake. She watched Robyn for a reaction. "He said he would come by one day next week and bring the final report."

Robyn concentrated on her cake and didn't seem to react to her words at all.

"I didn't get the impression he had much to report," Adeline continued. "Have you talked to him?"

Robyn looked up from her plate. "Me? No, I haven't spoken with him. Why?"

"Well, I rather thought you … I mean, when he was here last I thought you two might hit it off."

Robyn laughed in astonishment. "Why would you think that?"

"He seems like such a nice young man and …"

"I'm sure he is. He did ask me out that day, but I'm hardly in the market for … I'm not interested." They sat in silence for a while.

"You know, when I first met Albert, I was twenty-one years old."

There was a strange tone in Adeline's voice that made Robyn look up from her plate and study her expression.

"I had finished all the schooling available to me, and I was busying myself with charity work around the city, just marking time. My father was a wonderful man, but a very old fashioned one. He did not want me to be a professional woman. He kept my mother and me on a pedestal of sorts. We were to uphold the family and follow his orders. As the daughter of a wealthy man, there was little for me to do but wait to marry."

Adeline settled back in her chair. "Father was the director of railroads here in Dallas. Goodness, I don't know for sure how many lines there were then. I was very proud of him and my mother. She was a Van Patton, a well-to-do family back East. My parents were very prominent in Dallas society. I guess there weren't many suitors that measured up to my family's standing." She laughed softly.

"Albert was a clerk in my father's office. Gracious, he had any number of them. Albert had come up from Houston for his job, and somehow he caught my father's eye. Maybe it was just desperation on my father's part. I had no suitable prospects, I guess. I was facing old maidenhood." Adeline's eyes seemed to reflect a sadness that belied her smile.

"Anyway, one evening, unannounced, my father brought Albert home to dinner … I was completely captivated. He was tall and handsome and shy. But he was older than me by a few years and more worldly, more confident when it came to business, I suppose. He began to come to dinner quite often, and we would sit out there on the veranda and talk for hours. He was funny and smart. Like I said, I fell in love almost immediately. My parents were thrilled when Albert asked for my hand. He had no family heritage, no family at all apparently, but my father said he admired his ambition. We married there in the library, and we lived here while we were deciding where to build our own house. Albert was moving up in the company. Father was grooming him for leadership. It was almost a fairy tale existence." She paused and took a deep breath.

"But not quite. I don't know when I began to wonder about it. I was so happy at first, I couldn't see it. But gradually, I began to notice there was a dark sadness hovering around him. Not openly. He was kind and thoughtful to me, and affectionate. We had great times, many friends, but sometimes when he thought no one was looking, he looked worried, just weighted down with it, if you know what I mean. I tried to talk to him about it, but he would brush it aside, you know. It was the '30s. Everyone was worried. Times were hard—the Depression. Anyone working was just happy to have a job, always worried that they might be next. War was already raging in Europe, and the whole country was on edge, waiting for ... we weren't sure what."

"We had been married three years when Pearl Harbor was bombed. I'll never forget that day. Our whole world shifted. My father assured Albert that there was no need to enlist. He told him that the railroads were too important to the nation, and Albert would be exempt from military service. And he was. There was no need for him to go. No one would have thought less of him." Adeline paused, lost in her own thoughts for a moment. "Albert stayed at his job, but I could tell he was miserable. That cloud of sadness was growing. My father blew his top when Albert enlisted. He just did it one day, and then came home and announced it a dinner. Then he looked at me and said, 'I'm sorry, Addy, for letting you down."

"I saw him to the train the day he left. My parents wouldn't even come down to the station. And as I watched him leave, I had this foreboding that I would never see him again. He seemed almost relieved to be going."

"I spent the next two years blaming myself. If I'd been a better wife, if he had loved me more, if we could have had a child. I had failed. Why else would he give up our life here and go off to war when he didn't have to go?"

"And then D-Day came. His letters had hinted that he was to be part of something big. When I heard about the invasion, I knew he was in it. And then word came that he had been killed. The telegraph office sent a courier over. When I saw the boy coming to the door I almost collapsed. ... Everyone dreaded a telegram. I was a widow at twenty-eight. ... There were a lot of us." Adeline brought her hand to her breast as though even after all these years it was painful to say it.

"I held myself apart. The other girls, they had lost their men to war, but I ... I had lost mine because I had failed him somehow, and he had run away to war to escape me." She sat in silence for a moment, looking out across the back garden, gathering strength to continue her story.

"Then word trickled back of his bravery." She looked back at Robyn. "Albert had died a hero, saving the men who were with him. There were medals and commendations. Everyone reached out to me in my grief.. ... I was horrified at first. Afraid that others could see my failure, see that I had failed him as a wife. But gradually I began to see that no one else blamed me. They talked about Albert's sacrifice, his bravery. That he had chosen to go and fight for his country.

Everyone, especially my parents, just expected me to step forward and accept the honors Albert had won. No one blamed me but my own conscience."

Adeline paused again and looked down at her hands. Robyn sat stone still waiting for her to continue. Afraid that any reaction from her would disturb the moment.

"So, I began to build another story." Adeline looked up. "One that let me believe I had not driven him away at all. That Albert was a hero who had chosen to serve his country, and I was his widow who would not let the world forget." There were tears glistening in her eyes, but her voice grew stronger. "I hid my fears of failure. I would dedicate my life to honoring my husband. And as my sacrifice, I would not remarry, or have a family, or build a new life. My purpose would be Albert's legacy." She took a deep breath.

"The years flowed by, and I learned to live on my fantasies of perfect love cut short by war. The mantle of widow and family matriarch fit me well." Adeline smiled slightly. "Until a few weeks ago, when the truth came crashing in on me. I want to tell you the truth, Robyn, and then I'll never speak of it again"

"The reason my Albert carried his sadness with him, the reason I could never truly reach him, why he ran away to war, was not my failing as a wife, as I have feared for almost seventy years. He had his own secrets. Albert had another wife in Houston, a housemaid. And he had abandoned her when the chance to marry into my family wealth and position came along."

The shock of Adeline's words hung in the air and created a stillness that Robyn could almost reach out and touch. She held her breath, waiting for Adeline to continue.

"The first Mrs. Albert Sinclair died last February at

the age of ninety-six. I found out by a strange coincidence. She was alone, no children. Apparently she had spent her life in homage to her husband, too." Adeline smiled slightly. "To Albert's credit, he established a trust for her before he left for war. I'm sure he never worried about me with my family legacy."

"And so, I came to the truth. It was not my failure, but Albert's. He couldn't live with his deception. That was his sadness. The war offered him an escape. Would he have come home to me or to her? Or would he have disappeared completely and started again somewhere? He never got the chance to make that choice."

"I've never told a word of this story to another living soul, and I never will again. But I wanted you to know it, Robyn, because I see in you the same guilt, or debt I felt in myself. I don't know your experience, how happy you were in your marriage, or what you lost, but I do see you shutting yourself away from life. And what I want to tell you is, find a new purpose. Don't waste your life as I have. Don't waste your years trying to hang on to what you have lost. It's time to move on."

They sat in silence. Robyn's mind was racing over the story she had just heard. Guilt?

The guilt of being alive while Jonathon and the baby were lost. Was Adeline right? Was she hiding?

"I'm a meddling old woman, Robyn. But I've grown very fond of you. I'm not trying to marry you off, but that young man, that detective, he fancies you, I think. Go dancing, go out and meet some people your own age. Time passes very quickly." Adeline waited for Robyn's reaction.

"It's been almost three years," Robyn said after a bit. "And you are probably right. I'm hiding. I'm terrified. And I don't want to feel the guilt of being happy again." She brushed at the tears that were welling up.

"But you are very wise, Adeline."

Adeline smiled. "Well, end of lecture. I promise to mind my own business from now on."

Robyn rose and gathered her things. She walked around to Adeline and reached down to hug her. "Thank you for caring."

Adeline reached to pat her hand. "See you tomorrow."

"Tomorrow."

CHAPTER 28

Edwin Bennett's work suffered. He slipped in and out of his office like a shadow avoiding everyone. He couldn't handle questions right now. It was the same with his family. He feared that anyone who got a good square look into his eyes would see his guilt, and he didn't have time to explain or make excuses. He had to act, and quickly. Crazy, but he couldn't deal with this. It turned out he wasn't nearly as crafty and devious as he had always imagined. Greedy maybe, ambitious, but that was it. He couldn't deal with the deceit anymore. So, what was the worst that could happen? Adeline might write him out of her will? Shanks wouldn't give him a partnership? Was that it? Well, jail time and disbarment held a bigger threat. He knew what he had to do.

Murray Creed answered on the third ring. "Edwin! We haven't heard from you lately. Is there a problem?" And his voice didn't sound the least bit interested in the answer.

"Yes, well, I'm afraid there is. I just haven't been able to find the information you are wanting. You need to tell Mr. Cavander that I'm going to have to decline his offer."

Murray held the phone in silence for an uncomfortably long time.

"Are you there?" Edwin asked finally.

"I don't think Mr. Cavander is going to be in agreement with that."

"Well, I'm sorry. I told you I was afraid I couldn't help you. I spoke with my great aunt, and she has no knowledge of any papers either."

"You spoke with Mrs. Sinclair?"

"Yes."

Murray had no response for that news.

"Please tell Mr. Cavander that I appreciate his offer, and I'm sorry I couldn't help him out."

Edwin's palms were so sweaty he almost dropped his cell phone trying to close it. But step one was accomplished. Now step two.

Murray Creed stared at the phone after he hung up. This was not going to be easy to relay to the boss. He would need to craft his words carefully so that the blame didn't fall on him somehow. He worked out his presentation as he walked to Cavander's office.

Mitchell Cavander showed no expression at all as Murray talked. He just sat ramrod straight at his desk with his arms resting on the edge, and his fingers slightly touching. "He appreciated the offer?" His voice was just above a whisper.

"Apparently we underestimated our friend Bennett.

He told me he discussed our interest in the papers with his great aunt."

"Wonder if he mentioned the job offer?" Cavander smiled slightly. He took a deep breath and tapped his fingers together. "And he appreciated the offer, he said."

Murray nodded.

Cavander slowly leaned back in his chair. "How's the police investigation coming over there?"

As far as I've heard they have no suspects for the house or for the grounds."

"Maybe they need a little help. What do you think?"

Creed waited in silence.

"Why don't you let one of our sources make an anonymous call and give them our friend's name. Make things a little interesting for the good nephew."

"I'll take care of it right away," Murray said.

"Anything else?"

"No. Just stay up on the deal with Grayson Chandler. Keep me posted."

Murray walked away. That hadn't gone as badly as he had feared, not for him anyway. But Edwin Bennett was about to learn a hard lesson. No one says no to Mitchell Cavander.

Gladys came to the door, and it wasn't lost on Edwin that she opened it only slightly when she saw it was him.

"Do you think I could I talk to Adeline this morning?"

She opened the door wider and stepped back without a word or a smile.

I'm sorry I didn't call first, but I've been busy. I didn't know when I could get by here."

"She's in the sunroom having coffee. I'll bring you a cup." She disappeared through the dining room and left him to find his own way.

Adeline was hidden behind the newspaper when he stuck his head in the door. "Good morning."

She peered over the paper. "Edwin! Come in. I wasn't expecting you."

"No, I was out this way and hoped you wouldn't mind." He approached the table.

"I'll call Gladys ..."

"No, she knows I'm here. She let me in."

Gladys appeared with a cup and a fresh pot of coffee.

"So, to what do I owe this visit?" Adeline said with a smile. "You don't usually come so early."

"Or unannounced," Edwin said with a nervous smile. "But I have something to tell you, and I think the sooner the better."

Adeline frowned slightly. She could feel the tension from across the room.

Edwin cleared his throat. "There have been some things going on that you aren't aware of, but I want to fill you in. I'm no good at this intrigue business." He cleared his throat again as he settled in a chair. "Several weeks ago, in fact, it was the same day as my meeting with Grayson Chandler and your architect, Dalton Ramsey, I got a call from Murray Creed."

Adeline answered with a puzzled look.

"You probably don't know that name, but Creed is the right hand man to Mitchell Cavander. I think you have heard of him. He owns Vander Corporation. He's one of the wealthiest men in the world."

Adeline nodded.

186

Edwin took a deep breath. "Creed asked me to come to their office for a conference. I was, needless to say, excited at the prospect. I thought it had something to do with a real estate deal. But when I got there, it was sort of a tag team interview about my family history. Something to do with Henry Boll and another fellow from La Reunion Colony named Paul Henri. Have you heard of him?"

Adeline frowned. "Yes, he sounds familiar."

"The conversation centered around some journals that Cavander had come into possession of when he bought some property in Lancaster, out south of here. What Cavander and Creed wanted to know was did I have access to any records or journals from our ancestor, Henry Boll. Cavander said he wanted to compare the records of the two men, Paul Henri and Henry Boll, and fill in some gaps. Something like that." Edwin shifted his weight nervously in his chair.

I told him I didn't have any idea about family papers. Cavander said he was specifically interested in any records from the Civil War time period."

Adeline straightened her posture and drew back defensively.

"I know, it sounds bad, but please hear me out." He paused to see if she were going to allow him to continue. "I told them about the research that Barton & Ramsey was doing here, and that I didn't want to disturb that. He assured me that he knew about the research, and what he was looking for would not interfere. Then he tossed out a promise that I would be appointed his new consultant on real estate acquisition if I found whatever it was he wanted. I was stunned. That position would probably mean millions in retainer fees and ..."

"And a partnership," Adeline said.

"Yes, ... I have a family to think of. I ..." He grimaced. "No. No excuses. Bottom line, I agreed to check into it. It sounded harmless enough. I would just ask you. But ... and this is the part I'm not proud of, Addy, I decided not to tell you about it. Our relationship has been touch and go at best. I was afraid you would refuse. So I just ..."

"So you came over and feigned interest in the house."

Edwin had an expression of physical pain. "I'm not proud of this, Addy, but I'm trying to set things right." He took another deep breath. "Anyway, I came and saw the layout up there with the research. And I also saw I wasn't going to get anywhere. Cavander had put a deadline on it all, and my time was running out. So I panicked. I waited until about 3:00 in the morning, and I broke into your house." Adeline's expression did not change. She stared straight into his eyes and said nothing.

"I ... I did it twice actually. I was careful not to disturb any of the girls' work. I just wanted to find a journal or something from the Civil War time period. But it wasn't there." He couldn't look away from her stare, and he rushed on in his telling for fear she would stop him before he got it all out.

"In the meantime, my greed subsided a little, and I began to wonder what on earth Cavander was looking for exactly. He had mentioned something about Paul Henri's connection with a gun factory in Lancaster. A gun called the Tucker and Sherrard pistol. Then out of the blue, Creed called me and asked about any old buildings that might still be on your property. I told him I had no idea. But it got me thinking. Here he had me convinced whatever it was he wanted was in Lancaster; now it sounded more like he was interested in your house. That changed everything. He had said this didn't involve you here. So I went online to try and check some facts."

Adeline's expression had not changed. Edwin took another deep breath.

"I didn't find anything at first. You know you can wander around on the internet for days, there's so much stuff. But after my break-in was discovered and the digging, I looked again. I knew I had nothing to do with the digging out at the garage, and I also knew Cavander was interested in the grounds. It had to be him, and something had to be pushing him pretty hard.

I finally turned up what I was looking for on the computer. There's a mystery connected to the Tucker and Sherrard gun factory. It was in operation for about three years, but apparently the full order for guns was never delivered. What's more, the payment for the guns in gold bullion was supposedly sent, but never accounted for. I think Cavander found something in Paul Henri's journal that makes him think the guns or gold, maybe both, are buried here on your land. And I think he wants to find it before you do." He paused, almost surprised she had actually let him get the whole story out.

"I'm telling you this as a way of apologizing. There's no excuse for my actions. It was underhanded of me. You have every right to turn me in for breaking into your house. But I want you to know I meant no harm to you or the plans for your house. It was greed, pure and simple."

Edwin took another deep breath and waited.

Adeline blinked, it seemed for the first time since he had begun to speak. "You should have told me, Edwin." He nodded like a small boy caught misbehaving, but he didn't speak.

Adeline sat silent for several minutes. "So you think Cavander ordered the digging out there?"

That would be my guess. I have no way of knowing for sure."

"Does he know you broke into the house?"

"No. He might suspect it, but I've told no one but you."

"And, I believe Vander Corporation is one of the companies trying to buy me out. Is that right?"

Edwin nodded. "But I think this historical designation business had foiled his plans. That's probably what prompted him to speed up the search and enlist my help."

"I see. He needs to find the guns or gold or whatever, if they are here, before the preservation work begins."

"Right. That's my guess."

"And you took nothing away when you were here?"

"Nothing, I left everything just as it was."

The muffled sound of a knock came from a distance. Adeline looked toward the front of the house. "That could be my guest coming. I want you to stay, Edwin."

Gladys appeared at the door from the music room followed by Noah Garrison.

"Come in, Noah. I want you to meet someone. This my great nephew, Edwin Bennett.

Edwin, this is Detective Noah Garrison with the Dallas Police Department."

Edwin reached out to shake the hand that Noah offered. He was almost frozen stiff with panic. The police!

"Edwin dropped by unexpectedly this morning, but that's good because I'd like for him to hear your report."

"Certainly." Noah sat down next to Edwin. "Interesting that you are here today, Mr. Bennett. I wasn't aware that Adeline had any relatives in Dallas, but your name came up this morning."

"My name?" Edwin managed to say.

"Edwin is a real estate lawyer here in the city." Addy said.

"Yes, I got an anonymous call just before I came over here that you might know something about the break-in here."

"A phone call?"

"Yeah." Noah smiled. "You'd be surprised how often that happens."

"Well, I'm not very involved here at the house, Mr ... ."

"Garrison."

"Edwin is rarely here. I don't think he could help you much. Now what do you have to report today. Did you catch my intruder?" Adeline was obviously enjoying this very much.

"Well, I'm not too proud of this bit of work," Noah said. But basically, nothing has changed from the last time we talked. Our people did lift one footprint in the rose bed by the trellis, but there was no way to match it with the prints upstairs. Of course, that was before I got that phone call this morning." He looked at Edwin.

Edwin stared back. His heartbeat was banging in his ears.

"You know, Edwin, that could be your footprint." Addy said.

Edwin felt as though his heart had stopped!

"You remember you were out there last week." She looked at Noah. "I got him to trim the rose bush back for me. You remember Edwin? It was getting so rangy. You may have left a footprint in the bed."

Edwin nodded dumbly.

Noah studied his face for a few minutes. "So, you

don't have anything to add about the break-in. Any suggestions?"

"No."

"I'm sorry I forgot to mention the rose bush before, but I just remembered it now with Edwin sitting here." Addy smiled. "It's nice to have someone I can call on for little jobs like that. Edwin is very thoughtful."

Noah nodded. "Well, that explains our only clue, I guess. There were no fingerprints, nothing missing as far as we have determined. I don't like the idea of not knowing, but we will have to close the case, I'm afraid. I know that doesn't give you much security, and I'm sorry about that."

"What about the digging?"

"About the same. We've tried to track down this Ace Cable Company. There doesn't appear to be any record, except those two marker flags we found at the site. The tire tracks were no help. It was a truck, but other than that, it could be any truck with Michelin Tires."

"Maybe your phone person might be your suspect," Adeline said.

"You might be right, but there's nothing to go on, I'm afraid."

Adeline glanced at Edwin. "Well, we will stay watchful. That's all we can do, I suppose. I want to thank you for your efforts."

Noah nodded and then looked at Edwin. He stuck out his hand as he rose from his chair. "Nice to meet you."

Edwin scrambled to stand and shake his hand at the same time.

Noah turned to Adeline. "You keep my card now, and if anything comes up, anything at all, you call me. I might recommend that you install some sort of security. That would be a good idea."

"Well, as the restoration progresses, I'm sure that will happen. And I will call you if the need arises." Adeline extended her hand, also. "It's been so nice to know you."

Noah smiled. "I was wondering if Robyn Merrill is here today?"

"Yes, I heard her come in about an hour ago."

"I think I'll stop by and say hello, then." He smiled. "You take care now."

Edwin remained standing as the detective left. Then he turned back to Adeline and sank into his chair. She was studying him with a steady gaze and a slight smile.

"Thank you," was all he could manage to get out.

"Have you told me everything? No more secrets?"

"Everything."

"Then it's over." She paused for a moment. "We don't have much family left, Edwin. We have to stick together." She took a deep breath. "This Cavander person seems to play pretty rough. The next thing we need to consider is what would his next move be? How determined is he?"

"From my brief experience, I would say very determined and not very accustomed to losing."

"I think we need to include Grayson Chandler in our little circle. He needs to know about the offer they made you, and the history you have discovered."

"Whatever you decide. Tell him everything. I'm through with any intrigue."

"I'll call Grayson, then. Get him to come over, hopefully today."

Edwin nodded.

"In the meantime, there's something I need you to do for me, if you can."

"Anything."

Adeline rose from the table and motioned for him

to follow. I have a picture I'd like to have taken down in the parlor. Could you do that for me?"

"Taken down?"

"Yes. It's time for some changes around here, I think."

Noah's footsteps in the hallway alerted Robyn that a visitor was there, but she was surprised when he appeared at the door. "Good morning."

"You busy? I came over to report to Adeline, and thought I'd stop by."

"I see. Well, come in. I'll clear off a chair." She moved some papers while Noah surveyed the room. "No, don't trouble yourself. I can't stay long. How's it coming up here?"

Robyn straightened and folded her arms. "Slow and tedious." They both laughed softly. "So, what did your report say?"

"Hmmm? Oh, we're closing the file. Nothing missing, no clues to speak of. I mainly came over to apologize."

"Addy doesn't seem to be too disturbed by all this. She'll be fine."

"I guess I won't have an excuse to be interrupting you anymore. So I thought I'd give you one last chance to turn me down." He flashed that crooked smile again. "I was thinking I might take you to dinner this evening, if you're free. What do you say?" He waited for an answer, half expecting a no.

"I think that would be quiet nice."

"You do? That's great! Say seven o'clock?"

"Perfect. Do you need … ?"

"I have your address. I'm the police, remember?"

"Right. Seven it is."

Noah slowly backed out the room. "See you then."

CHAPTER 29

Grayson Chandler was no one's fool. He knew if he wanted to work in this town, it would be unwise to get on Mitchell Cavander's bad side. But Adeline exhibited a strangely negative reaction when he called her about Cavander's offer.

"I'm not sure I want Vander Corporation involved here," were her exact words.

"Well, unfortunately, they are already involved. Cavander owns the land on your southern boundary. Any decisions made for the area are going to include them."

"I'll deal with that later," Adeline said. "That's not what I need to talk to you about. I have something more important. I was about to call you. I need you to come over this afternoon. Can you do that?"

"I'll clear my calendar." Grayson smiled as he put down the phone. When Adeline requested something, he would make it happen.

Adeline was waiting in the sunroom when Grayson got there. She motioned for him to sit down. "I had an interesting talk with Edwin this morning. He'll be back shortly, and I'll let him explain it all. After you hear what he has to say, you may see things differently. Would you like something to drink?"

"No, I'm fine." Grayson settled back in his chair. "So you and Edwin are speaking again."

"Yes, well, I don't have that many relatives, you know." She smiled. "I can't afford to run anyone off at my age."

They sat in silence for a few minutes.

"It sounds like the plans for the house are progressing," Grayson ventured just to fill the quiet.

"Yes, the girls have some success. Hopefully they'll find the records soon."

They both looked toward the front of the house when they heard the door open and hurried footsteps across the entry. Edwin rushed into the room like a person on a mission.

"Sorry, Adeline. Traffic." He shook hands with Grayson and sat down. All the swagger and defenses he had exhibited in their last encounter were gone, Grayson noted.

"Edwin has something to tell you, Grayson. I'll just let him do that. I want you to hear him out, and then we need to talk."

Grayson nodded and waited for Edwin to speak. Whatever he had to say, it seemed the relationship between Addy and her great nephew had changed. He got the feeling that they were now on the same team.

Edwin began where he was leaving the meeting

with Grayson and Dalton Ramsey, the phone call from Murray Creed, and his meeting with Mitchell Cavander. Grayson listened with rapt attention, as did Adeline. Edwin glanced at his great aunt from time to time, and she responded with slow nods of encouragement. Yes, the dynamic between them had most definitely changed.

Edwin got to the part of his story covering the break-in. He apologized again, this time including Grayson.

Adeline added in the part about the young police detective, and Grayson had to stifle a smile over Edwin's discomfort, but Edwin didn't seem to notice. He was deep into explaining his internet journey. Grayson's attention perked up when he got to the part about the guns and the gold.

"So you're telling me that Mitchell Cavander was responsible for the trespassing incident at the old barn."

"I'm just saying I have good reason to believe it was him. I can't say for certain, but everything else I'm telling you is cold fact." Edwin paused and waited for a response.

"Eight hundred four thousand in gold?"

"Possibly, maybe more, maybe less. And who knows what the guns might be worth. It's enough that Cavander is apparently willing to step over the line a little."

Grayson took a deep breath and looked at Adeline. "Well, this might explain Cavander's sudden burst of civic spirit for funding the restoration here."

Adeline smiled. "You see my reservations".

"Yes." Chandler looked at Edwin. "So, where do you stand with Cavander now?"

"Well, apparently not so well. I called Murray Creed and told him I couldn't help them. I declined the position. Then when I was here talking to Adeline, this police detective shows up and tells me he had just received an anonymous call suggesting I was responsible for the break-in."

"Sounds as though you ruffled some feathers."

"Exactly. Cavander doesn't like the word NO."

"What did you tell the detective?"

"I didn't manage to say much under the circumstances." Edwin laughed softly. "But Adeline saved me." He explained about the rose bed.

"Quick thinking," Grayson said.

Adeline smiled. "So this is where you come in. We wanted to make a clean breast of it all and get your advice."

"I see ... well, first off, do you believe the gold and guns story is true?"

"Maybe" Edwin offered. "Point is, Cavander seems to."

"Well, you could take a chance, and let him fund your project. He could spend a bundle out at the old barn and find nothing." Grayson laughed softly. "That might give you some satisfaction, Edwin, since he apparently tried to get you arrested."

Neither Edwin nor Adeline looked as though they thought that was a good idea.

"Course it would also make Cavander the good guy for his civic spirit and quite possibly, he'd find what he's looking for."

Grayson paused and thought for a bit. "On the other side of this, you can turn him down flat and make him even angrier. Then you risk what his next stunt might be. In the meantime, he could cause all manner of trouble to slow up your restoration work."

Adeline frowned. "You believe he could really do that?"

"Most certainly. Trust me ... maybe for now we need just to stall until the historic designation is awarded. Cavander will hold up on trying to stop the research because he'll be hoping to get his deal in place. Once the award is made, there isn't much he can do. Cavander has no idea that you stumbled on to this guns and gold mystery. Right?"

Edwin shook his head. "No, it's never been discussed. As far as I know he thinks we're still in the dark on this."

"Well, then let's go with that. Let him think we have no idea what he's up to. None of this leaves this room. Even Ramsey or his people. Understood?" Adeline smiled and looked at Edwin. "You see why I keep this fellow around?"

Edwin smiled. "Even a lawyer needs a lawyer from time to time."

"So for my part, I will ignore this stunt with the police and pretend that I'm still considering his offer?" Adeline asked.

Grayson nodded. "As far as Cavander knows you are very pleased that he's taking an interest, and you are just waiting on the award to make your decision."

Grayson called Murray Creed after he got back to his office and explained the situation. Murray was a little set back by Grayson's stalling on their offer.

"It seems to me it would be advantageous for Mrs. Sinclair to have her funding set before the historic designation was finalized."

"Yes, but the thinking is that if we began the work on our own, it might create legal problems down the road. Mrs. Sinclair is very appreciative of the offer, but she wants to wait until we've heard from the certification board. I'm sure you can understand. In the meantime, I would like to go ahead and set the meeting to discuss your offer on the Boll property.

"Certainly. When did you have in mind?"

"I'll let you discuss that with Mr. Cavander."

"I'll get back to you."

Grayson smiled as he hung up the phone. Yes, some feathers might be ruffled, but no threats were made, and that was often the case in dealing with Cavander, if he had heard correctly. But, just as he had thought, Cavander was frozen for now, trying not to disturb his chances.

CHAPTER 30

"Okay, now the test." Noah said as they left the restaurant. "How do you feel about jazz music?"

"Jazz music?"

"Yes, I put everyone through this. How do you feel about listening to jazz?"

"Everyone, as in all of your dates?"

"Only the ones I truly want to impress." He smiled that crooked smile.

"Well, I suppose I would say that I like jazz. I'm not an authority or anything, but I can recognize it when I hear it. Does that count?"

"By all means. Willingness to listen is very important. I was thinking that I'd take you to my favorite spot for listening."

"I'm all for it."

"It's in Deep Elm. Do you know that area?"

"A little. My sister lives down there. But I've only seen it in the daytime."

"Ah, then you are in for a treat. It changes a lot after dark. ... What do you mean your sister? I didn't realize you had family here."

"We aren't that close, actually. Long story."

"Right. Sounds like my family. So, we'll go for some jazz." He pulled into traffic and crossed to the inside lane.

Robyn watched the city flow by her window. She was having a wonderful time. Noah was fun to talk to about almost anything, it seemed. He was interested in just about everything in Dallas from sports to theater. He even liked to read. They compared book favorites and found they liked some of the same authors. She had not felt this comfortable talking to someone in a very long time.

The club was called "The Red Door," and was just glitzy and sleazy enough to be a nightclub. The place was packed, but they managed to squeeze into one of the last table spots in a back corner. They stage whispered their drink orders back and forth with a waitress and settled in. The band was on stage, and the spot light was on a tenor sax player. He finished his solo and the audience applauded. He acknowledged them with a nod as the music drifted on to the next musician.

Noah leaned close to her ear. "The guy up front there is a friend of mine."

They sipped at their drinks. "Best thing about jazz fans," Noah whispered, "is that they actually listen to the music."

Robyn looked around at the crowded club. It was a total mix of people. Some looked much like them, dressy casual, and others looked as if they could be hanging out with Shelby. Then a thought struck her. Shelby might even be here. Wouldn't that be weird?

The band finished the set and took a break. The

noise from all the conversation folded in around them. Robyn saw the sax player step off the stage and begin to make his way through the tables, stopping to talk to different groups.

"Jax!" Noah held his hand up to get the man's attention.

The musician saw him and came over. "Noah, my man! How you doing?"

"You sound good tonight, bro." He turned to Robyn. "This is my friend Jax Preston. Jax, meet Robyn Merrill. I'm showing her the town tonight."

The man called Jax smiled and extended his hand. "I think we've crossed paths before."

The light of recognition flashed for Robyn. "You're Jax. I should have recognized the saxophone." They both laughed while Noah looked puzzled.

"We almost met one day," Jax explained. "She was looking for Raven and knocked on my door."

Noah frowned. "You know Raven?"

"My sister." Robyn explained.

"She's here, somewhere. "I'll get her." Jax scanned the crowd, then waved someone over.

Raven, all in black, topped in red, worked her way through the tables. Robyn had a sinking feeling as she saw her coming. This was probably not going to go down well.

"Hey baby; look who's here."

She saw Noah first and smiled, then noticed Robyn, and her look changed to shock.

"Hi, Shelby."

Shelby just glared. "It's Raven."

"So you two are a little surprised, I guess," Noah ventured.

Jax pulled up two more chairs and motioned for Raven to sit down. She did so, reluctantly.

"Well, this is interesting," Jax said. "How did you two meet?"

Noah explained about the break-in at the Boll Mansion and Robyn's connection.

"I heard something about that," Jax said. "You okay over there now?" He asked Robyn.

"Fine, no more excitement."

"One of my boys mentioned something about that," Jax told Noah. "I was going to call you."

"When was that?"

"Yesterday. I was over at the center working with the group. Poppy brought it up. Said he knew something about a job that went down over on Swiss. I'd seen the note in the paper about the house. It might be connected. What are you looking for?"

"Nothing, really. We closed the case. Nothing was broken, nothing missing. It was just trespassing. No leads."

Jax shrugged his shoulders. "I'll see what the kid says next time I see him. Could be nothing."

Noah leaned over to include Robyn in the conversation. "Jax volunteers at the community center. Teaches music for free to inner city kids."

"So what do you think of the show?" Jax asked.

"Wonderful. I love the saxophone."

"All right!" He looked around at Raven, who was slumped in her chair with her arms crossed, glaring at Robyn.

"So you two work with youth groups together?" Robyn asked.

"Well, not so much together," Noah said. "I'm in the athletic part, and Jax takes care of the music."

"Noah, here, coaches everything from soccer to volley ball. Beginner to semi-pro, I think."

"They're a little short-handed most of the time."

The two men laughed good-naturedly. "Where are you holding classes now?"

There's an old warehouse on Harwood. It's no palace, but it has a roof and four walls."

"There's a shortage of cheap space downtown." Noah explained to Robyn.

There was motion at the stage. Jax looked up. "I have to get back to work. Good to see you, man, and nice to meet you officially." He smiled at Robyn and shook Noah's hand. Then he stooped to kiss Raven on the cheek as he left.

There was an awkward silence with the three of them left staring at one another.

"So, did you and the folks have a wonderful time?"

"You got my notes?"

Raven nodded slowly. "I got'em." There was that smirk Robyn had wondered about.

"Mom and Dad were disappointed they missed you."

"Yeah, well that's what I do best, you know." The conversation died.

Robyn looked at Noah. "Did you see a restroom sign?"

Noah pointed behind her. "Back there."

Robyn rose and squeezed through the crowd at the bar. The hallway was brightly lit in contrast to the rest of the club. She squinted against the glare and was about to push the door to the ladies room when Shelby/Raven caught up with her.

"What the hell do you think you're doing here?"

Robyn turned in surprise. "Shelby, this is ridiculous."

"Raven! My name is Raven, damn it! What are you doing crowding in on me. Isn't it enough you made my childhood a living hell? Why can't you get out of my life!"

Robyn watched the meltdown in amazement. Shelby looked like her old self—a four year old child in full tantrum mode.

"I'm sorry," she heard herself saying. "I had no idea where Noah was taking me, or that you would be here."

"Yeah, right! You have the whole town, and this is the spot you just happen to pick."

"I had no idea you would be here. No idea that he and Jax were friends. I ..."

"It's the same old thing, big sister. You're so innocent, so righteous. You make me sick!"

A couple of slightly drunken girls rounded the corner searching for the ladies room, stopped in surprise, and then squeezed by them through the door.

"Shell ... Raven, I don't know what I've ever done to you to deserve this kind of outburst."

"Like hell you don't!"

"But if you feel this strongly, just go back to the other side of the room and forget I'm here. My date brought me here. It isn't my doing. He wants to listen to the music. I'm not going to ask him to leave."

"You know damn well what you have done, sister."

Robyn folder her arms defensively. "Well no, actually, I don't. For the life of me, I've never understood. And at this point in our lives, I guess it doesn't really matter. We just need to stay out of one another's way."

"Exactly! And away from Jax! All smiling and charming and coming on to him! I thought you were going to come over the table after him!"

"That's totally not true! I just ..."

"And you can shove your superior attitude, sister dear! Talking down to him like that, like you're better than him."

Robyn stared in stunned silence.

"Oh, I can see it. Judging Jax, judging me. You can't wait to rush back and tell our parents ...."

"Tell? Tell them what?"

"All my life, there you were. Miss Perfect! I ..."

"Wait a minute. This is it? Your big chance to tell me exactly what I've done to you that is so terrible, and all you can come up with is that I'm perfect and that somehow segues into me flirting with Jax and then judging you. That's it?"

"Mom and Dad worshipped ..."

"They worshiped us both, Shelby. But you couldn't see it. Why else would they have put up with your horrible behavior all these years."

Raven paused for a moment in her rant as if to summon new strength. "I want you out of my life. Stop spying on me."

"For once, little sister, we agree. This is it. I'm never apologizing again. You better find some other purpose for your life besides suffering my existence, because the matter, Shelby, or Raven, or whoever you are, is over! Now excuse me, I'm trying to get to the bathroom." And she escaped through the door.

When she came out Shelby was gone. Noah was sitting by himself enjoying the music. She sat down and glanced out over the crowd, but Shelby was nowhere in sight.

"You okay?" Noah asked.

"I'm fine." She forced a smile. "He's very good, isn't he?" They listened to the rest of the set in silence.

⚬⚬❯⟨✕⟩❮⚬⚬

"Well, that was a little more excitement than I had planned for tonight." Noah said after they were in the car. I'm sorry I got you into that."

"Hey, how could you know I had a psychopathic sister down here. Could you hear her?"

"Oh, yeah."

Robyn cringed. "I'm so sorry."

"Not your fault. Not your fault. Do you want to talk about it?"

"Not really. I think I'm through talking about it, or thinking about it, ever. This takes the cake. I can't fix it. I'm walking away."

Noah nodded and looked at her out of the corner of his eye as he drove. They rode in silence for a while.

"So you and Jax are very involved with the inner city youth programs."

"Yeah, I feel like the attention I give those kids through sports might keep them from showing up on my police report down the line."

"Good plan."

"I met Jax through that program. He's great with kids. Maybe that's how he can handle your sister." They laughed.

"Again, I'm so sorry about this tonight. I don't normally generate this much drama in my life."

"Well, I hope not! I was beginning to think I was going to have to make an arrest back there for disturbing the peace, or the club, or whatever." Noah smiled that crooked smile.

Robyn cringed, too embarrassed to respond.

"Hey, don't feel bad. The last time my family got together for a reunion it wound up in a fight that sent three people to the hospital."

"Really?"

"No." Noah cut his eyes around in a gesture that looked like a little boy caught in a fib. "But there was a big argument over potato salad. Does that count?"

Robyn smiled. "Well, then I guess I shouldn't feel so bad."

"Right, we can't pick our families, you know. They are forced on us at birth … Now you can pick your friends, though. That is the good news, and I think I'm picking you, if that's okay."

Robyn smiled. "Yes, that's okay."

"Good, because if you're going to be my friend, then you have to come to see my teams play."

"That sounds like fun."

"Great! It's a date. We have a game Saturday, actually. I'll pick you up at eight-thirty."

"In the morning? That's my day to sleep in."

"Yeah, well, not this Saturday."

CHAPTER 31

The rest of the week went smoothly enough. Robyn thought it was surprising really. Normally, the encounter with Shelby would have hung over her head for days, but she hardly thought of it at all. Instead she felt light, happy, as though a weight had been lifted. Maybe it was because she had finally had enough of her little sister. Watching Shelby's meltdown in that club brought back all the memories of the times she had used those same tactics to reduce Robyn to tears. Guilt that maybe she had in someway hurt or cheated or misunderstood whatever the situation might have been. But watching her sister in the glare of those hallway lights had finally hammered the truth home. She could not fix the problem. Shelby was the problem, seeing slights and plotting in every event. She was through with Shelby, and the feeling was liberating.

Or maybe it was just Noah that had lightened her mood. The thought of him caused her to smile. Adeline was correct. She had been hiding. But enough was enough. Jonathon would never leave her heart. The baby would never leave her heart, but she had to move on. Noah was a fresh wind in her life, and she found herself doing something she had not done in a very long time. She was looking forward to the weekend. She tackled the files with renewed energy.

In the back of one of the drawers, wedged at one corner, she found a heavy tag-board binder, the kind with the flap and string tie. She tugged on it to break it free and lifted it out. It was fairly heavy and was obviously going to take a larger space on her desk than was clear now. She balanced it on her lap and started to carefully look through the pages. The house. This was it! The original drawings, the 1889 plans, blueprints, figures, materials. Luis Boll, bless you and your filing obsession!

"I've found something."

Mary stopped what she was doing and came over to look.

"It's the house." Robyn smiled up at her assistant. "We need to get these papers to the office, secure them so that they don't get damaged, make copies of everything, catalog everything."

"Should I go tell Mrs. Sinclair?"

"Yes, go down and tell Gladys and Adeline. Tell them we are headed back to the office. I'll gather everything up and be down in a second."

⁘⦃⧓⦄⁘

But Adeline was napping when they asked for her. Gladys promised to tell her as soon as she awoke. Robyn and Mary rushed back to the office with their prize. Ramsey was going to be very pleased.

It would take days just to separate the pages and

unfold the plans so they could be photocopied and protected. Everything was there, elevations of the original house from all sides, detailed sketches of the 1889 construction, the 1924 library addition, measurements, descriptions of materials. It was a historic preservationist's dream.

The final additions to the proposal would be added, and the application submitted. The question now was how to proceed. Could work begin without disturbing Adeline? Would she agree to start the work or even be willing to move out for a time? Or would all this be on hold until after she was gone? It was up to Adeline. Whatever her decision, the most important step could be accomplished. If the house could be saved from destruction, all else could wait.

CHAPTER 32

Robyn enjoyed the game. Well maybe not the early hour, or the wind. How could it blow like that on the soccer field and be so calm everywhere else? But she enjoyed the game itself and watching Noah interact with the boys. The kids were all sizes and shapes and rather scruffy looking in their mismatched shorts, but their team shirts that Noah handed out were crisp and sharp looking; warning sign orange with black numbers. The eleven-year-olds played with enthusiasm and pride. They lost by one goal, but Noah emphasized all the positives and told them he was proud of their effort. After a round of snacks, the boys peeled off their shirts and carefully put them in coach's bag before they melted away into the surrounding neighborhood.

Noah gathered the equipment and shirts while Robyn watched. "This way I can be sure they have their jersey for the next game," he explained. "These guys are pretty much on their own out there. Laundry isn't high on their list." He shouldered the bag and smiled. "Now. Was that good? Did you enjoy it?"

"Yes. Very much. I thought you were going to score again there at the last."

"Better luck next week. You should have seen us last season. We've come a long way."

They walked to the car. "If you don't mind, I have one more stop. I need to go by the league office right quick and pick up some papers. It will only take a minute. Then we can go find some food."

"Whatever you say."

"It's right around the corner."

The office, as Noah called it, was a small one- story building that had probably been a convenience store at one time. Squeezed in between an auto repair shop and a second hand store, it looked drab and temporary.

Noah held the door open for her. "Excuse the mess. We move a lot so we work out of boxes here."

A cardboard sign announcing "Greater Dallas Community Services" was stuck haphazardly in the frame of the glass front door.

The front office was empty, but they could hear voices whose owners were out of sight. Noah guided her back to an area where papers were stacked on several tables.

"Hey, Noah. How's it going?" A woman called out from the other side of the room.

"Hello, Carter. I was just going to pick up the forms for basketball."

"Right on that first table there. Boys or girls?"

"Both."

"Ah, an ambitious man." The group of women around her paused in their work of sorting papers and laughed good-naturedly.

"This is my friend Robyn." He gestured toward her. "The rabble over there would be the volunteers around here."

More laughter. Greetings were exchanged.

"Well, thanks. See you Wednesday night at the league meeting."

"Right." The talker looked at Robyn. "Nice to meet you."

Robyn nodded. As they left she got the feeling she was probably going to be the next topic of conversation.

"Now, your reward for being a trooper and coming out at the crack of dawn on a Saturday morning."

"Yes, let's get to the reward part."

"I was thinking Café Brazil. How does that sound? Have you been there before?"

"No, I haven't."

"Then you are in for a treat."

The café was crowded with interesting groups of people—students, workout groups, and other people like them with the windblown look of an early morning soccer field. The motif of the place was "college campus coffeehouse" decorated in local art. Most of it looked like someone's class project work. Colorful would be a good description and very welcoming. Robyn smiled when she saw the place. She was truly falling in love with her new city. They made small talk over Noah's recommended choice: a wonderful cheese omelet smothered in tomatoes and avocados.

"So how many kids are involved in your sports program?"

"Probably a thousand or so, boys and girls from

six to sixteen. Well over that if you include basketball too. Course, lots of the kids play both, so I don't have the exact count."

"Wow! That's impressive."

"It's a good program. Completely free to the ones who fit the profile. Most of those kids are in foster care or living with a relative, or single parent homes that just don't have the time or money for them. Lots of their parents are in prison, or just messed up with drugs or alcohol. The coaches and teachers are all volunteers like me. We're more interested in providing a positive environment for them than we are producing winning teams, but ..." He smiled that crooked smile. "Winning's good, too."

"How are you funded?"

"County and city charity funds, individuals, bake sales, whatever we come up with."

"What's the problem with your location? You said you move a lot."

"It's hard to find cheap rental space downtown, and that, of course, is where we need to be. A developer comes in and improves an area. That's good, but the rent then goes up. We have to go find something cheaper. It happens all the time, but we just work out of boxes and adjust."

"I'm very impressed, Mr. Garrison, with your organization and with your own commitment."

"You are? Well, good. That was what I was going for by dragging you out here this morning. Because I was hoping I could impress you enough that you would have dinner with me again tonight, and I promise we won't go to Deep Elm."

CHAPTER 33

Edwin Bennett, Dalton Ramsey, and Adeline Sinclair listened intently as Grayson laid out his idea. It sounded reasonable. Three big players bidding on the property; three companies each with a large stake in the surrounding area. Why wouldn't they welcome a tax write-off in the midst of this deal?

The three companies, Penrow Corporation, Vander Corporation, and Andover-Warren would each buy one-third of the Boll property, excluding the house and immediate grounds, at market value, then donate the land to the city for a community park. Whatever investment they were sinking in the deal would be partially offset by the deduction. Adeline Sinclair would donate her house on the condition that she could live there for the rest of her life, at which time the house would become part of the park.

"I've talked at length with Andover-Warren and with Penrow and they are both considering it." Grayson said. "I'm waiting on a call from Murray Creed for a meeting with Cavander."

"Something like this has been done before," Edwin said. "I think they will go along with it. The park will enhance the surrounding building projects they are planning, and the tax write-off helps their bottom line."

"Of course, then there's the question of price." Adeline said. How much do you think my land is worth?"

The men all looked at one another as if each were waiting for the others to answer. Grayson spoke first. "That's an interesting point. Land in this area is priced by the square foot. Your property is virtually in downtown, so the price is substantial"

"Give me a figure."

Grayson nodded toward Edwin. "I believe commercial real estate is your field."

Edwin smiled and took a deep breath. "Well, let's see. You have a little over twenty acres here. One acre is 44,560 square feet. The land in your area is selling for about $35 a square foot. If you do the math on that, one acre would be worth a little over one and one-half million dollars. Then, of course, the twenty acres would push that up to a little over thirty million."

Adeline sat in stunned silence while the men waited for her reaction.

"It's overwhelming, isn't it?" Edwin said after a bit.

"As I said before, the contract can stipulate that you can live here undisturbed for the rest of your life." Ramsey said. "We can go forward on the restoring of the house in ways that would not disturb you. The roof, the exterior, shoring up the foundation possibly. You will be in control of that."

"This sounds too good to be true," Adeline's voice was a whisper.

"Yes, it does, but in this case, it is true," Grayson said. "If the three companies agree to the plan, it can all come true."

"When will you know?"

"Hopefully, in the next few weeks."

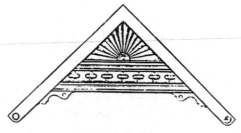

CHAPTER 34

Dalton Ramsey liked to get to the office by eight each morning, then have a few quiet minutes over a cup of coffee to get ready for the day. Usually he and Mira were the only ones there that early, and they quietly ignored one another for a while. Waiting for him on his desk was a list of calls to return. Apparently the feelers on possible design jobs for the Swiss Avenue projects were bearing fruit He was reading down the list when Robyn stuck her head in the door.

"Got a minute?"

"Sure, come in. You're early this morning. What's on your mind?"

Robyn studied him with a slight frown. "I have an idea. I want to bounce it off you."

"Shoot." Ramsey leaned back in his chair and motioned for her to have a seat. Robyn perched on the edge of a chair as if she were preparing to make a run for it if the conversation didn't go well.

"I've been thinking about uses for Adeline's property. I think I may have a good idea."

"Let's hear it."

"A friend of mine is involved with the Dallas Community Services program. They run an extensive outreach program for inner city kids through sports and the arts."

"Yes, I'm familiar with the group."

Robyn nodded. "Well, it seems one of their big problems, besides funding, of course, is that they don't have a permanent home. They need cheap housing for their offices and that's hard to find and keep downtown."

Ramsey nodded.

"I was thinking, what if Adeline's home and the other houses we want to preserve were turned into office space and activity space for non-profit groups? There must be a lot of art and social outreach programs like the Community Services Group that could benefit. Adeline's house could be used as a community event center for all the groups, or more office space, whatever." She stopped abruptly and waited for Ramsey's reaction.

"That's a good idea." Ramsey stared off into space a second. All the other buildings we add could be in the turn-of-the-century style. The park could have a 1800s theme to it." He started writing on a pad in front of him. "A band shell, ball fields, walking trails, everything in period style. This is good. This is good. Have you written this up in proposal form?"

"No, I wanted to talk to you first,"

"Right. Well, you need to get all this down. Brainstorm, try to think of all the aspects of the design. You can present it to the next staff meeting and ask for input. I like it. It's original. Good work."

Robyn smiled from ear to ear.

"Well, get cracking! We have another design meeting on Friday. That gives you two days. Let me know if you need any other people to help you."

"I'm on it!" Robyn rushed out of the room with Ramsey calling after her. "Tell Mira what you need, and she'll set you up."

Grayson had never been to the offices of the Vander Corporation before, and he had to admit the setup was impressive—the private elevator, the luxurious furnishings.

Murray Creed met him at the elevator and escorted him to Cavander's office. Both men were gracious and professional. And short. He felt like a giant.

"I'm glad we can have this meeting today." Cavander said as he settled behind his desk.

"Yes, I've been meeting with the people who are interested in the Boll property. I'm sure you are aware that Penrow and Andover-Warren are also bidding."

"Yes, I believe we all have investments in the area."

"I have a proposal for you that I think you might find satisfactory."

Grayson explained the plan while Creed and Cavander listened intently. "Both Penrow and Andover-Warren are considering the idea. Their initial response was very positive."

"I see your point," Creed said. "This might be a good option. With the size of investment we are committing to the area, we will be looking at a lot of possibilities."

"Of course, real estate development is not the main interest of our company," Cavander said. "It's only one element of our organization."

"I understand. I know you only recently invested in the land you have there. But a commitment of this size is going to require cooperation with the other companies. A green belt project at the center would benefit all of you, I think."

"How is the possibility of our participation in the renovation coming?" Cavander asked. "Has Mrs. Sinclair given that any more thought?"

"Well, I think she still is waiting on the historic designation to be approved. That is, of course, her priority."

Creed and Cavander exchanged glances. "Well, Grayson, I'll take your idea into consideration. We'll need to get some figures on this. See how much capital you are talking."

"You'll need to put together some sort of meeting of the three companies for an agreement to be reached," Creed added.

"And I think you might talk to Mrs. Sinclair. See if she would be willing to agree on our involvement. Maybe we could tie her interest and ours together in this," Cavander said.

"I see." Grayson studied the serious expressions on both men's faces. So here was the threat. Vander Corporation would stall the deal until Adeline gave them what they wanted.

"I'll talk to her and explain the negotiations. Also, I would like to set up the meeting of the three interested companies."

"Just let us know. We'll be willing to talk."

The men shook hands as Grayson left. He had a clear picture now.

"I'm not moving. You can start with the repairs on the exterior of the house. That won't disturb me, but I'm not moving." Adeline sat forward in her chair and tapped the table for emphasis. "I don't want to delay this, Ramsey. Let's be realistic. I probably don't have all the time in the world left, and I want to see this through, if possible."

"I understand. But realize there may be some major repairs needed. I can't promise ..."

"We'll deal with any problems as they come up. I'm not moving."

"Very well. The second thing we need to talk about is financing. I'm sure Grayson told you about Mitchell Cavander's offer to underwrite some of the work, but ..."

"I'm not sure I want Mr. Cavander involved at this point. You need to talk to Grayson about that."

"I see. Okay, then the third thing I wanted to discuss with you is the house structure itself. We've studied the plans. The core of the house is, of course, the original farm house, built of limestone. The building plans show that the original house was built in the French style. It had a cellar. Apparently, it was closed off when the 1889 addition was added. Were you aware of the cellar?"

"No, I'd never thought about it."

"Here is a copy of the drawings we have." He laid one on the table and turned it to show Adeline. "Before we make any other adjustments or renovations for the house, it would be advisable to check the foundation integrity."

Adeline studied the drawing and then glanced up at the word integrity.

"We need to examine the foundation of the central house. The cellar may have been filled in when the new structure was added, or it may be just sealed off. We'll make sure the foundation is in good repair before we do any other renovation. It would also give us a chance to reinforce the original flooring."

"What would that entail?"

"Well, apparently, the entrance was through a hatch at the back of the house. That would be under your sun porch here. We'll need to take up this flooring and look."

Ramsey waited for Adeline's reaction. "Of course, that is going to be disruptive. That's why we wanted to give you the option of moving out for a while."

"That wouldn't disturb the rest of the house though." Adeline frowned.

"No, but it would inconvenience you and Gladys." Ramsey looked around at the sun room. "I know you use this area a lot."

"We'll just move into the parlor. That should do, wouldn't it?"

"Yes, it should."

"Very well. When would the work start?"

"As soon as you want."

"The sooner the better."

Ramsey folded the drawing. "Then it's settled. I'll get a contractor lined up right away."

Adeline smiled. "It might be interesting to see what's down there."

CHAPTER 35

Noah Garrison caught himself humming softly as he worked. He quickly cut it off and looked around to see if anyone had noticed. His area of the station house office was clear. He was safe. He smiled. Noah, old boy, hold it down. Coming off like a love-sick school boy would not be good for an on-duty cop. He sat back in his chair and stared out across the top of the surrounding desks. That's what he was all right. Robyn Merrill was the best thing that had happened to him in a very long time. He had vowed after his first mistake of a marriage to stay single forever, but ... Robyn was different. And he couldn't quite figure her out yet. There was a reserve about her, a reluctance to let him get to know her. He didn't want to rush things and scare her off. He needed to go slow.

Noah shook his head as if to clear it. He smiled again in disbelief at his own thoughts and tackled the report before him. The phone on his desk rang only once before he picked it up. "Detective Garrison here."

"Noah, How you doing, bro?"

"Jax. I'm good. What's up with you?"

"Well, I told you I'd get back to you after I talked to Poppy."

"Poppy?"

"The kid I'm working with. Good little horn player. You know, I said he had mentioned something about the break-in on Swiss Avenue."

"Oh, yes, I remember now."

"Well, I got a chance to talk to him yesterday after practice. Poppy is a good kid, but he's on the fence, if you know what I mean. He could go either way."

"Yeah."

"I asked him about the thing on Swiss. He said yeah, he knew something. Said a dude picked him and a friend up over on Bryan a few weeks back and offered them twenty-five dollars each to help him out for an hour or so. He gave them each a t-shirt to put on and drove them over to Swiss. Had this big white dually truck with a sign on it."

"Did the kid remember the address?"

"No, just a big house on Swiss. Front entrance through a hedge. Poppy said they drove off the road, out across a field, over to an old rock foundation. The man told him and his friend to hold up some kind of sighting equipment and then help him measure off the foundation. He stuck a few little flags in the ground and used a gadget to drill down in several places like he was looking for something."

"What did he come up with?"

"Nothing. Poppy said just dirt. He placed it in plastic bags and labeled them. Took a few pictures, and that was it."

"What happened then?"

"Said they loaded everything up, pulled up the flags,

and left. The man stopped over on Grand Avenue and let them out. He paid them and asked for the shirts back."

"That's it?"

"Poppy said they watched him go. When he got to the next alley entrance, he stopped and tossed the shirts in a trash bin and drove off. Poppy said those were good shirts, so he and his buddy went down there and fished 'me out."

"Very good. Does he have the shirt now?" "Yeah, he had it on. It has Ace Cable printed on the front. Poppy said that's what the truck said, too."

"Do you think the kid could ID the guy?"

"I don't know. He might, or he might just clam up on you. You know? He's got a brother doing time. Poppy doesn't trust anyone, if you know what I mean."

"What's the brother in for?"

"Gang shooting. He was in a carload of punks that shot up that club last year. Some kid on the street got killed. Little girl."

"Yeah, I remember that."

"Poppy's different though. He's trying to stay clean. He's got a chance, too. He's good on his trumpet."

"Well, tell him he's in no trouble and see if he would be willing to come in and look at some pictures."

"Yeah, I'll do that."

"Thanks for the call. This is the best information I've gotten so far."

"No problem. Say, good to see you the other night."

"Yes, good to see you."

"That girl, Raven's sister, you still with her?"

"Yes, I am."

"Good for you, man. Sorry that went down the way it did."

"Yeah, we sort of got caught in the cross fire there."

They both laughed.

"Raven's cool most of the time. Maybe we'll be seeing you again."

"Maybe. You never know."

"I'll talk to Poppy and get back to you."

"Thanks for the call."

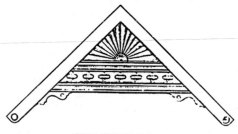

CHAPTER 36

The contractor's crew sealed off the sun porch from the rest of the house and pulled up the floor. It didn't take long. Ramsey and Robyn came and joined Adeline and Gladys to watch. The old hatch to the cellar was still there waiting invitingly. It was sort of like opening an old tomb, Robyn thought, as the workers carefully lifted the doors. The hinges protested but they worked. Stone steps led down into a black space. The contractor rigged a light and led the way. Ramsey followed him down while Robyn, Adeline, and Gladys peered over the edge.

"It's not filled in." the contractor called up.

"Not much here," Ramsey added "Watch your head if you come down."

Robyn descended the steps. The air was musty and still. She ducked her head to avoid the low beams of the ceiling. The area was about the size of an average room. In one corner sat a wooden bench and next to it, a crockery churn. A shelf down one wall still held several jars. Pieces of wood, scattered at random across the floor appeared to be parts of an old chair.

"Well, mystery solved. Nothing of interest here." Ramsey said.

"The walls look pretty good, though," the contractor added. "They've held up pretty well."

"Look them over good and let me know. You might check these floor supports also." He reached up and tapped the beams just above his head.

"Yeah, we'll need to brace all this up and reinforce the floor beams just to be sure the house is sturdy."

Robyn and Ramsey climbed the steps to where Gladys and Adeline were waiting.

"Anything?" Adeline asked.

"Very little," Robyn said. "Here's one of the jars I found. There are a few more down there on a shelf."

Adeline took the jar carefully and stared at its contents.

"I just never thought about anything being down here." Gladys said. "It's sort of eerie really, thinking about the vacant space right under our feet all these years, and we never knew."

Ramsey took Adeline's arm to guide her up the workman's ramp and into the house.

"It looks good down there. I didn't see any major flaws in the foundation. That's good. We want to have a solid base for everything."

"Did he say something about replacing the floors?" Adeline asked.

"Only reinforcing them. We have to keep everything as the original to meet the requirements of the historic marker."

"Good."

"Robyn and I have something we want to share with

you. I brought over a proposed plan. I'll let Robyn tell you about it."

"Wonderful. Let's go to the dining room where we can spread everything out."

Ramsey rolled out a large map of the property on the dining table.

"We've been working on this for some time, as you know," Robyn said.

Gladys and Adeline studied the layout while Robyn explained the idea. The design group had approved her idea and come up with some additions. The map in front of them showed Adeline's house and grounds along Swiss Avenue. Robyn explained that the house would be refurbished and restored as a part of the park area. Other houses, built in a style that matched the Boll Mansion, would be added as office space for nonprofit organizations. Adeline's foundation would maintain the buildings and new offices. The grounds around Adeline's house would be landscaped, and the map showed picnic pavilions and a bandstand. The larger area held walking trails, playground equipment, and game fields.

"The park will be the center of the development in the area. The invested companies are planning space for high rise apartments and small commercial businesses.

Organizations such as the Historical Society, or Big Brothers and Big Sisters, music societies, community outreach programs, and sports programs can qualify for office space." Robyn looked up at Adeline. "Eventually, your house will be opened as a community center for weddings, receptions, and festivals. We can envision art shows and historical displays being housed here." She fell silent and waited for Adeline's reaction.

Adeline studied the map carefully. She ran her hand slowly across the park area and stopped at her house. "This is wonderful." When she looked up she had tears in her eyes.

"We had some discussion about a name for the project," Ramsey said. "We researched other locations in the city and discovered that even with all the projects you have sponsored over the years, you've never put your name on any of them. This one, I think, should be yours. Our committee chose Adeline Boll Sinclair Park. Is that acceptable?"

"Yes, I suppose it is time for that," she said in a low voice.

Gladys put her arm around Adeline's shoulders and gave her a hug.

Ramsey's cell phone rang. He flipped it open and listened for a moment and then smiled at the women. "That's great. I'm with Mrs. Sinclair now. I'll tell her the news."

He closed the phone and winked. "We got it! That was Mira. It will take some time for the paper work to clear, but I've got a friend on the board. He just called to say it's been approved. This house is now protected as a historic structure."

CHAPTER 37

Mitchell Cavander was furious when he heard that the Boll Mansion had received its designation as a historic building. Creed brought him the paper as soon as Cavander entered his office. The two men were silent as Cavander read the article, and that silence continued for a time after he finished; Murray waiting for his boss's reaction, and Cavander racing through a series of thoughts. Creed had witnessed this many times before. It was one of Cavander's signature traits, almost a childish reaction to defeat. It was a grown man's version of a temper tantrum, not unlike holding his breath until he turned blue.

"And she's still holding me up on the damn funding." Cavander blurted out. "How can she do that? The cost is going to start mounting and ..."

"Actually, she promised to make a decision once the certification came through. Maybe this is the news you've been waiting for."

Cavander stopped in mid rant and considered the idea. "Right, maybe so. Get her on the phone, or rather get that lawyer of hers."

Grayson was expecting the call. He had already warned Adeline, and they had worked out a response. Cavander's threat was clear. They had to let him get involved at some level, or the entire deal could fail. So when the call came, he was ready.

"Yes, we were very pleased to get the news. Everything is falling into place it seems. The Barton & Ramsey people have created a development plan, and we're ready to go to work."

"So Mrs. Sinclair approves of our involvement?"

"Certainly. We just need to get together and work out the details. I was going to call you. The people from Barton & Ramsey are going to set up a meeting. They have to get their presentation in order."

"That's fine. Let us know." Creed looked up at Cavander as he spoke. They exchanged a smile, and Creed took a deep breath of satisfaction. Crisis averted. The boss would have his way.

Jax came with Poppy to the station house. Noah shook the boy's hand and thanked him for coming. Poppy was nervous. His eyes had that wide-eyed on-alert look of someone in fear of surprise attack. He kept glancing at Jax for reassurance.

"Thanks for agreeing to do this. It will really help us."

"Hey, no problem." Poppy scanned the room quickly.

"First off, had you ever seen this man that hired you before?"

"No, man. He just drove up in that big old truck."

"What exactly did he say to you?"

"He just asked if we wanted to make a little money for about an hour's work. We asked him, doing what? And he said surveying. He said he'd pay us each twenty-five dollars."

"So you agreed?"

"Yeah, man. Why not?"

"So you got in the truck with him. Can you tell me anything about the truck?"

Poppy considered his question for a moment. "It was white, big old king-cab dually, brand new."

"Why do you think it was brand new?"

"It didn't have nothing in it, man. You know, nothing on the dash, nothing in the floor. Brand new."

"Did the truck have any markings?"

"Just this." Poppy opened his jacket to show his shirt front. "It had one of those magnet signs on the door. You know, you can just stick 'em on and take 'em off. And it said Ace Cable, just like my shirt."

"What about the man? Can you describe him?"

"White dude, maybe thirty or forty,. ... old."

"What about his looks—hair, clothes, like that?"

"He was bald. Looked like he shaved his head and he had on brand new work boots. Didn't look like they had ever touched the ground."

"Glasses?"

"Shades."

"Anything else?"

"He had a tattoo on his arm."

"Upper arm or lower."

"Upper. You could just see it down below his shirt sleeve."

"Was it a prison tat?"

"No, man. It was pretty bold. Cost some money, I would guess."

"And was he wearing an Ace Cable shirt, also?"

"Yeah."

Noah added to his notes. "Okay now. We're going to look through a few pictures, and see if you spot anyone." He flipped on the computer and brought up the program. He started with known felons for breaking and entering. Poppy studied the faces as he clicked through them. But after thirty minutes of photos, he had seen no one that caught his interest.

Noah switched over to another category. When he was setting up for the interview, he had tried to imagine all the types who might fit this profile. It didn't seem to be a situation that would attract men with records of violent behavior. More than likely just petty theft and burglary suspects. Or one other category—private investigators. That might be a possibility. He opened the file on registered investigators and flipped through the pictures.

Poppy studied the photos, shaking his head after each one, until about five minutes into the series. "There's the guy." He smiled in triumph and looked around at Jax for approval.

"You're sure?"

"Yeah, that's him. I forgot about the mustache, but that's him. Who is he?"

"He's a private investigator named Collin Baxter."

"A cop?"

"No, a private eye."

"Like on television?"

"Yeah, like on TV."

"How about that?" Poppy looked back at Jax. "That's good, man. I don't want no trouble."

"Jax clapped him on the shoulder. "Good job."

"Is that it?"

"That's it. You can go." Noah shook the boy's hand.

"See, that wasn't so bad." Jax said as the two walked away.

"Yeah, that's good. Man, I was afraid some crazy ex-con would come after me, but ..."

"So see, you have nothing to worry about, and you did a good thing."

Noah stared at the screen. A private eye? Now who would have hired him? He checked the address listing.

CHAPTER 38

The next few weeks slid by quickly. There was much work to do in planning. Great care had to be taken before any work could start. It was important to protect the original materials where possible. Robyn was hard at work on the detailed layout. She loved this part of her job. It was where imagination and engineering technique came together. This project was particularly satisfying. One, because she had become so personally involved with Adeline, and two, because it included both buildings and landscaping. And with the process of analyzing the materials in the house—matching paint and brick, restoring the woodwork—it was a pleasure to contemplate.

"You got a minute?" Mary was at her office door.

"Sure, come in. What's going on?"

"Well, I've been copying layouts of the original 1858 construction, and I have a question."

"Let's hear it."

"I was helping Jeffery out at the house yesterday. He was marking the locations so they can install the floor supports in the cellar. We measured the area, and came up with fifteen feet wide by twelve feet long.

"Yes?"

"Well, I was looking at this copy I just made of the

original sketches. It shows the cellar to be fifteen feet wide by sixteen feet long."

Robyn processed the numbers for a moment. "Let me see that." She studied the sketch. "Where's that extra four feet?"

"That's what I'm wondering. I remember that we found that receipt about repair on a foundation."

"That would be odd, though, to do the repairs four feet out from the original wall." They stared at the drawing for several minutes. "Let's go talk to the contractor."

Nathan Fields was the man in charge of the work on the house. He was in the cellar when they got there. The floor was marked where the new support pillars were to be placed. They showed him the drawing. He stepped off the length of the cellar and then frowned. "You're right. This doesn't match up." He patted the wall. "It's solid enough." He shone a light on the ceiling beam above his head. "But look up here. This wall stops at the flooring. The flooring should be pegged into it, not the other way around. This is not a support wall. It was added after the floor was in place above."

"How does that affect the structure?"

"Well, we'll have to take down enough of it to figure out its purpose."

"I'll call Ramsey and let him know."

It was several weeks before Noah was able to follow up on the private investigator lead. He had to work it in on his own time since the Boll case had been closed. He drove out to the address he had on Collin Baxter. It was just off Lemon and Lovers, an older apartment district that was beginning to show its years. He walked in past a pool area that had seen better days. The manager's office was on the end, and a man came to the door wearing a red apron that said, "Dog Meister."

Noah identified himself. You could tell a lot about a neighborhood by how someone reacted to a visit from the police, he had learned. Apparently Lemon and Lovers had nothing to hide. The man was very pleasant.

"Come on in. I just lit the grill on the patio. I've got to watch it."

Noah followed him through the apartment.

"The wife's still at work. I'm in charge of dinner tonight," the man called back over his shoulder. The grill was blazing and they watched the flames die back down. "Have a seat. I'll let this get going good." Noah chose an aluminum chair covered in basket weave strips of green plastic. The man did the same.

"Now what can I do for you?"

Noah explained who he was looking for, but the address was no good.

"Baxter moved out several weeks ago. He got a job offer in Belize. Said he'd be down there a year, so he let his lease go."

"Do you have any way of reaching him?"

"No. He didn't give any new address."

"What about his mail?"

"You'd have to talk to the postman on that. I think he is in the complex right now."

The man walked out with him to locate the mailman.

But the postman was little help. "He filled out a card

and asked me to turn it in. No forwarding address, just asked the Post Office to hold his mail. He never got anything personal much, anyway."

"Never?"

"Just flyers."

"Did you talk to him often?"

"Just that one time, really, when he gave me the card. I usually never saw him."

So, dead end there. Noah thanked the postman and the complex manager and walked back to his car.

There was a tiny bar crammed in between the apartment houses advertising happy hour from four to six. It looked like a place his man might frequent.

Inside there was just enough room for a counter and two tables. He showed the bartender his badge and asked if he knew Collin Baxter.

"Yeah, he's a regular. Or he was. He moved away not long ago. Said he had a job out of the country."

"Did he say where?"

"Yeah, probably, but I forgot."

"Was it Belize?"

"Yeah, I think so, sounds right."

"I need his help on an investigation I'm conducting. You don't know how to get hold of him do you?"

"No, sorry. Baxter was kind of a quiet guy. Kept to himself. It's the business he's in, I guess."

"Do you know who he worked for?"

"He was independent I think. Took jobs as they came up. He did a lot of work for big companies."

"You have any idea which ones? I might be able to track him down that way."

"Vander Corporation was one, I think. Some fellow was in here one night complaining about that company, and how they'd cheated him somehow. Baxter spoke up and told him to forget it. He said Mitchell Cavander didn't make his money by making friends, and he was good at making enemies. Something like that. Made me think he knew quite a bit about that company."

"I see what you mean. Well, thanks for your help. If you see or hear from him, tell him I'm looking for him." He handed him a card.

"Will do."

Robyn called Ramsey on her cell phone and told him about the wall and what the contractor had said. "He's got the equipment here now if you want to take a look."

"I'll be right over. Tell him to go ahead and set up to take the wall out, if he can.

By the time Ramsey got there, the construction crew had put in some large jacks against the ceiling beams to take any pressure off the wall. Nathan Fields handed out safety glasses and hard hats to Ramsey and the girls. "If you're going to stay down here, you'll need these."

The slabs of limestone came out fairly easily after the workmen sliced through the mortar with a power saw. They removed the stones carefully one at a time. Robyn noted that the removal had no effect on the ceiling. This was definitely not a load-bearing wall.

After a few minutes, the contractor shone a light into the cavity, and they all peered in at a canvas sheet draped over a square-edged mass. They pulled a few more stones out, and Fields lifted the canvas covering to reveal stacks of small wooden crates. Written across the end of each crate were the words

Tucker & Sherrard Arms Factory
Property of the CSA

"CSA," the foreman said. "What's that?"

"Confederate States of America," Ramsey said. "Looks like Civil War materials of some sort." He reached in and brushed some rubble away. "You might go get Adeline, Robyn. She needs to see this." The workmen took a break, and they all stood staring at the hole in the wall.

"Someone didn't want these to be found." The contractor said after a bit.

"Let's just hold up a minute until Mrs. Sinclair can get here."

It took some time for Robyn and Adeline to come. Gladys came, too.

"I called Grayson." Adeline said as Robyn helped her descend the steps. "And Edwin also. They're on the way."

"You don't seem too surprised by this." Ramsey said.

"More than you would think." Adeline smiled.

By the time Grayson and Edwin got there, which didn't take long, Ramsey noted, the workmen had cleared more of the wall. There were twelve boxes in all. The whole group just stood and stared at them for a while.

"Were you expecting this?" Ramsey ventured to Grayson.

"No, not exactly. We had heard a rumor."

"So what do we do now?"

"Well," Grayson looked at Adeline and Edwin. "I think we need to get some sort of team in here and move these cases to a secure location." He flipped open his phone and made a call. "I think I'll get a better signal outside." He went up the steps to the back garden.

"The group milled around while they waited.

"What do you know about this, Adeline?" Ramsey ventured after an awkward silence.

"Nothing. I've never heard a story that included anything like this."

"But Grayson said he had heard rumors."

"That was in the last few days. Before that, I had never heard anything."

"Where did Grayson learn the rumors?"

Ramsey saw Adeline and Edwin exchange a quick glance. There was a long pause before she answered. "I suppose you have to ask Grayson about that." And her tone carried the message that she wanted no more questions.

Ramsey acknowledged her warning with a nod, and silence fell over the group again. And when Grayson came back, Ramsey asked him nothing.

It took a couple of hours for the armored truck to arrive, and the crates to be moved. They placed each one in a separate tray to ensure that the movement didn't damage the boxes. The last two crates were slightly different in size and bore no writing at all. Adeline, Edwin and Grayson glanced at one another as the last crates were successfully transferred, but still they didn't comment.

Grayson gave the driver instructions, and they watched the truck leave.

"OK, now, let's hear it." Ramsey smiled. "You three

246

look like you are about to explode."

"Let's follow that truck first. This is going to take a while to tell." Grayson said.

Grayson, Edwin, Ramsey, Adeline, and Robyn were there when one of the crates was opened. They were secured in the safety deposit area of the First Trust Bank.

"Let's just take a quick look. We won't open it completely." Grayson said.

When one slat of the box was lifted, oiled rags burst out of the confined space. Grayson lifted the cloth and the glint of gun metal met their eyes. Staggered in neat rows were pistols, large bulky revolvers.

"How about that?" Ramsey asked. "Is this what you expected?"

"They look to be in pretty good condition," Edwin said.

"How many are in the box?" Adeline asked.

"Looks like about twenty."

Ramsey saw Adeline and Edwin exchange looks again.

Ten cases," Grayson said. "Two hundred pistols in all, and very little corrosion due to the oiled rags they were packed in apparently; that and the air- tight crates."

"How much do you think these are worth?" Robyn asked.

"My guess would be between ten thousand and fifty thousand a piece depending on how badly a collector wanted one. I checked the records and there are only four known to exist other than these," Edwin volunteered.

"So you were expecting this." Ramsey said. But again he got no reply.

Robyn did some quick math. "That's between two and ten million dollars!"

"Exactly."

The group stared at the final two unmarked boxes.

"I guess this is as good a time as any." Grayson said. He used a hammer and chisel to pry up one corner of one of the cases. Stacked neatly, row on row, were bars of gold. He pulled the top of the case back so that the group could see it all. There was stark silence until Ramsey ventured. "How much do you think is in there?"

"Maybe around 300 ounces in each box." Edwin said. Everyone looked at him. "I've been doing my research," he said.

"What about ownership?" Robyn asked.

"Well, according to the antiquities law, I believe possession goes to the property owner. Since these cases have been lost for more than one hundred years, I think the law would apply."

"Same for the gold?"

"That's my understanding. Of course, there will be taxes."

Edwin produced a calculator and pressed in the numbers. "That's approximately six hundred ounces of gold at say twelve hundred dollars an ounce?"

"That's about right."

"That's something over seven hundred thousand dollars."

The group stared in stunned silence.

"So, who hid these crates?" Ramsey asked. Grayson shook his head. "No idea."

"Henry Boll?"

"He was away for most of the war. He was in the

Confederate army," Adeline offered.

"And, if it were Boll, wouldn't he have recovered this after the war?" Robyn asked.

"He died in 1904. Wouldn't he have taken this out at some time?" Ramsey ventured.

"Paul Henri was the one in charge at the Lancaster Gun Works." Edwin offered. "He may have hidden them."

"In Henry Boll's house?" Ramsey asked. "It's the same question again. Why didn't he recover them later?"

"Yes, Paul Henri lived more than twenty years after the war." Edwin said.

The group was silent, at a loss for explanation. "We may never know," Adeline offered after a bit.

"Well, regardless of the mystery, I would say this takes care of our funding issues." Grayson said, and everyone laughed nervously.

Dallas 1865

Zebediah turned the team down the road to the south. The sun was full up now. He could hear the sounds of the farms around him waking up. Cows lowing in their pens waiting to be milked. The shuffling hooves of horses as they were harnessed to the plow or the wagon. The storms from yesterday had rumbled on toward Red River. It would be a sunny day today. In the distance the village of Dallas lay under a smear of wood smoke. People would be out now and might wonder where he had been so early.

Zeb took the left fork in the road and skirted the town. Best to stay away from folks this morning. He would cross the Trinity as he had last night, just above Dowdy Ferry on the limestone shallows. Boss Henri would be waiting at the yard. He would be glad to see him this day.

As he neared the north bank of the river, he saw

riders ahead. Four men spread out across the trail. A spike of warning curled across the back of his neck, and he sat straighter on the wagon seat and gripped the reins tightly. He didn't want no trouble. No sir. But it could happen, him alone like this, without his master. And no papers. It could happen.

The riders reached the south bank of the river at the same time Zeb's team set foot in the water. The men stopped to water their horses on the far side. Only one of the men seemed to notice him. But he stared clean through him it seemed to Zebediah. The riders were blocking his path. He hauled on the reins. There was nothing to do but wait.

The man watching him said something to the others in a gravely voice, and all four men looked his way. They were travel worn and disheveled, and there was something military in their look.

Fear spiked up Zeb's back. He should have turned off the road as soon as he saw them. He should never have come down to the river. The men were raiders. He could see that now. But it was too late.

The men flicked their reins and moved their horses toward him now. There was nothing for him to do but watch.

"You lost, boy?" One of the men rested his hand on the pistol shoved in his belt. He made a comment under his breath and the others laughed with a cackling sound.

"I'm talkin' to you, boy. Are you lost?"

The men reined up on either side of his wagon. He could see their eyes now. See the rage in them.

"No, sir, I ain't lost. I'm almost home."

"Almost? You sure? You sure you didn't just steal this here team and wagon and run off this morning?"

"No, sir. I'm working. I'm taking this wagon home

251

to my master this morning."

"That right? Now just who do you belong to?"

"Master Argyle Tucker. I work at the foundry over there in Lancaster."

"Is that right?"

"Yes, sir."

"What's your boss man doing letting you wander off like this?"

"I'm working. Yes sir, I'm just on my way home."

The man stared at him with a hard look, while one of his companions checked the empty wagon bed. "Nothin' here."

The man spat a wad of tobacco into the river. "Well, boy, when you get home, you tell your people that this is your lucky day. You hear me?"

Zeb sat frozen in place. Fear buzzed in his ears and paralyzed his thinking.

"Will you do that?"

"Yes, sir."

"You tell your people you just met Quantrill's Raiders this morning, and they let you live."

The other three men doubled over in laughter, and their horses milled and splashed. Zeb's team strained against his hold and jerked the wagon forward.

"You tell 'em, now."

"Yes, sir."

The four riders heeled their horses and began to move up the bank.

"Quantrill's Raiders." The man called out again. "You tell 'em that."

Zeb listened as the horses moved away behind him. He signaled his team with a flip of the reins and crossed the stream. His heartbeat was hammering in his ears. "Quantrill! Sweet Jesus, protect me!"

His team made the south bank and scrambled up the incline. He wanted to run. Slap the reins and set those horses moving! Get clear of the river. Get as far from the men as possible, but the grade was steep.

He never heard the shot. It struck him in the back of the head. He pitched forward and crumpled into the wagon box at his feet. Then there was silence as the team continued to move on, down the trail toward home.

The rider on the ridge across the river watched as the slave slumped over. He smiled at his companion. "There now, you owe me five dollars."

"Yes, I do." The man slapped him in the shoulder. "That was a crack shot, partner. I never thought you could do it."

CHAPTER 39

Dallas 2007

Grayson and Ramsey met in the parking lot on their way into the meeting with the participating companies. Ramsey looked at his watch. They had fifteen minutes. He tried to shift his thoughts from the discovery of the guns and gold to the presentation he was about to make, but this had been a busy day.

"I had an interesting phone call this morning before all the excitement came up." Grayson said in a low voice.

"Really? Your day sounds as confusing as mine." They laughed.

"It was from Noah Garrison, the detective on the break-in investigation."

"I thought they closed that."

"They did, but Mr. Garrison seems to be taking a personal interest."

"Has he found something new?"

"He said he thinks he knows our trespasser."

"Really? Is he going to reopen the case?"

"I'll fill you in after this meeting. I can only fight one fire at a time."

They were laughing softly as they entered the meeting room.

Cavander and Creed were both at the table, as were representatives from Penrow and Andover- Warren. Ramsey's presentation on plans for the park land and the Boll Mansion went smoothly, and from the nods around the table, it was well received. Next Grayson Chandler took over to explain the business deal they were proposing. He offered the price of thirty-five dollars per square foot for Adeline Sinclair's property if the companies would agree to partner on the buy and then donate the land. The full price of the twenty acres would be slightly more than thirty-one million, and that amount would be split three ways. He also emphasized the tax advantage this would afford each company and the contribution they would be making to the city.

"How would the actual development of the park and its maintenance be funded?" the man from Penrow asked.

"Good point. The house will be the responsibility of the Adeline Sinclair estate. The park grounds will be part of the city park system and be under their maintenance. Also, we have already had offers of assistance from the private sector. And, there has been a development just in the last few hours that will most likely ensure that the park project will be well funded."

Cavander and Creed were listening intently at this point.

"What would that development be?" one of the Andover-Warren people asked.

"It would be premature to go into too much detail

just yet, but there was a discovery at the house today. It all needs to be evaluated fully, before we make an announcement. But I feel confident in saying that if you underwrite this park project by donating the land, you can be assured that the park itself will be maintained in a manner that will be a long term benefit to your surrounding buildings."

Cavander shot a glance at Creed. They've found them! The others at the table nodded in response to Chandler's report and then read over their copies of the prospectus on the table before them.

The man from Andover-Warren spoke up. "We have discussed your advance information on this. I'm authorized to say that my company will agree to these terms if the other parties agree. The Penrow representative spoke softly to his partner and then cleared his throat. "I can make the same commitment for Penrow." Everyone in the room turned to look at Mitchell Cavander.

Cavander whispered something to Creed but he did not make eye contact with the other men at the table. Creed straightened in his chair and took a deep breath. "I'm afraid that Vander Corporation is going to need further clarification on this before we can agree. Elements here that have been introduced at the last few minutes have raised questions."

"Then ask the questions," the Penrow man said. But Cavander was already standing. Creed gathered his papers and joined him. "We wish you every success, gentlemen."

And the two walked out. Cavander was stiff with anger and did not have a word to say.

The rest of the group stared in amazed confusion. Then they looked to Grayson.

"Give me just a moment," Grayson said, and he followed Cavander and Creed out of the room.

Cavander looked back and saw Grayson following them. He stopped abruptly and turned on him. "I don't like to be blindsided, Chandler! I won't be party to these underhanded dealings!" He was stumbling over his words in his anger.

"There's no attempt to blindside you. You indicated that you wanted to be part of the renovation of the Boll property. That's still in place."

"And what's this nonsense about valuable artifacts?"

"I don't believe anyone said anything about artifacts, Mitchell. But I have had quite a few surprises today, and some of them may be of interest to you. Now if you will hear me out, I think we can clear this up." He motioned toward a small conference room off the hall.

"Absolutely not! You can talk to my lawyer in court."

Creed stepped between the two men and leaned in to whisper to Cavander. "Let's listen to what he has to say."

Cavander glared at Creed and then Grayson, but he stopped talking. "Five minutes," he said after a bit.

Grayson closed the door on the room and faced the men. "I had an interesting phone call from the police department this morning. It seems they have the identity of our trespasser at the Boll Mansion."

"And why should that concern me?" Cavander shot back.

Grayson studied him for a moment, and let the silence do its work. "I think we both know how the identity of the people surveying on Mrs. Sinclair's property might concern you."

Creed started to speak, but Cavander cut him off.

"Whatever you are implying, I'll bury you in the

courts. We both know that."

"And I, Mr. Cavander, can bury you in the news-papers."

Mitchell Cavander glared at Grayson, but he held his tongue.

"But, I believe you have a plan to offer," Creed spoke up. "Otherwise you wouldn't have followed us out of the meeting."

"Yes, I do. And if you'll hear me out, I think we can come to an agreement. The question is, Mr. Cavander, why did you get involved in this project in the first place? What is it that you want in this deal?"

"We want the situation resolved without further confusion." Creed spoke quickly, before Cavander could respond.

"I can guarantee that the trespassing case will not be reopened unless an effort to reopen the break- in investigation is made." Grayson let his words sink in for a moment. "Now here's what I want. I want the full cooperation of Vander Corporation on this park proj-ect. I want your company to join with the other two in buying the Boll/Sinclair property at the agreed price and donating the land for a park as we outlined today."

"And exactly why do you think I will be in agree-ment on this?" Cavander shot back.

"Mr. Cavander, you are a powerful man. It will do my client or this project no good to have you for an enemy. But from your standpoint, you must consider that you already have a large commitment in land here. It is to your benefit, as well, if we can work this out. What I want is for you to leave here happy with the outcome."

"Well, you aren't doing too well, so far."

"Yes, but I have something in my possession that I think you greatly desire."

The Dallas Morning News ran the report of the new development planned by Penrow Corporation, Andover-Warren, and Vander Corporation as the lead article. The three companies were praised for their contribution on this latest project for the city and especially the donation of land for a park complex to further enhance the uptown area.

Mention was also made of Adeline Sinclair, a long time patron of the city, who was offering her historic home as centerpiece to the park.

Right below the lead article, a shorter piece reported the finding of Confederate weapons hidden in the Boll Mansion.

> "... The reason that the guns and gold were hidden at the house or who might have hidden them there remains a mystery, and the full value of the find is yet to be determined.
>
> An undisclosed number of gold bars were also found with the weapons.

The article went on to name the Tucker and Sherrard Arms Factory of Lancaster, Texas, as the manufacturer of the guns.

> "The copies of the Colt 44 Dragoon, made during the American Civil War, were found in their original packing and in good condition.
>
> The guns were described as valuable to collectors. Only four of the weapons were known to still be in existence before this discovery was made."

Gun experts were quoted as saying the pistols were possibly valued at over ten thousand dollars each by collectors because of their unique history and scarcity.

Grayson Chandler, spokesman for the Adeline Sinclair estate, reported that most of the cases of weapons will not be opened to prevent exposure to the atmosphere and possible corrosion. The cases have been x-rayed to reveal their contents of twenty pistols and powder flasks each.

One case showed signs of being opened previously, and two pistols and powder flasks were missing. Mr. Chandler stated that it is unclear when the pistols were removed, or where they are now. Representatives from Texas State Archives have been invited to view the artifacts.

CHAPTER 40

Dallas 2009

The Adeline Sinclair Park project was shaping up nicely. Two years of careful planning and hard work had transformed the neighborhood into an uptown triumph. The stately new buildings developed by the three companies were almost all completed, and they looked down on this jewel of a park. The eighteenth century accents to the buildings and quiet tree shaded grounds were an attraction for the inhabitants of the new high rise apartments and condominiums.

Gladys Thornton had proposed the grand opening date of April 28th, Adeline's birthday. As Adeline would have said, it was a 'glorious' time of year with a rainbow of flower blooms and the new greenery of trees and shrubs splashed across the grounds, and yet no hint of the summer heat to come.

Robyn parked her car by the Boll Mansion and walked across toward the bandstand area. The renovation of the house was proceeding smoothly. It would be open to the public in another year. The foundation had reported to her that they were already receiving bookings for receptions and recitals a year in advance. And of course there had already been one wedding in the library.

People were scattered like colorful confetti across the lawn, busily setting up booths and displays. All the nonprofit groups which had established offices were represented. Many groups from the surrounding buildings were there, also. The park was turning out to be just as, Adeline had hoped, the heart of a community.

On the bandstand, Robyn could see the director of the concert talking with the sound engineer. Jax Preston waved as she approached. He had organized a full lineup of bands to perform today, from his student groups to headliners from local clubs.

"How's it going?" Robyn asked as she got within voice range.

"Looking good." Jax gave her a thumbs up.

"Have you seen Noah?"

"He's over at the playing field helping set up games, I think. Have you talked to Raven this morning?"

"Yes, she said she was coming over early with you."

"We got here about an hour ago. She's over at the arts and craft area."

"Looks like we'll have perfect weather for the art show outside."

"We will if Raven has any say in it." They both laughed.

Robyn went to find Noah. This fund raiser/grand opening was all his idea. Great way to celebrate and honor Adeline, plus a good way to promote and fund the community groups, he had said.

And it was. Besides, only Noah could have managed to include so many groups, and only Noah could have talked Raven into her part as the art show organizer. It fit perfectly with her career, as she had gained a respectable following in the arts community. Maybe not so totally counter-culture anymore.

It still amazed Robyn that she and her sister had reached some sort of truce. And with Jax and Noah providing the venues, they had gradually found some peaceful common ground. Like Adeline had counseled, family is important. She and her sister might never be close, but what they had achieved was close enough to bring their parents some pleasure.

Noah smiled and waved when he saw her approaching. Then he reached out to give her a quick kiss when she drew close. "How you doing, Mrs. Garrison?"

"Wonderful," she answered.

"Looks like a beautiful day in the neighborhood, and we're going to have a good turnout."

"One of your better ideas, Mr. Garrison."

"I don't know now." He flashed that crooked smile. "I've had some pretty good ideas lately." He winked.

On stage the band played a fanfare to get everyone's attention. From all directions around the park people began to flow on to the green expanse. Robyn turned in a slow circle to take it all in. Adeline would have loved this day. She pictured her friend in her lovely mauve silk blouse and skirt and that spectacular pearl necklace, smiling with delight. Adeline had lived long enough to see the park open, the grounds all restored, and last Spring's flowers covering the beds. That was something at least. And she had celebrated her ninety-second birthday in her own home, knowing that it would be safe and appreciated for the years to come.

Edwin Sinclair Bennett and his family came on stage in her honor, and Gladys Thornton cut a ceremonial ribbon to open the festival. Also on stage, Jax recognized representatives from Penrow, Vander, and Andover-Warren Corporations for their part in development of the park. Dalton and Diane Ramsey, representing Barton & Ramsey as the designers of the buildings and landscape, waved to the crowd. Jax reminded the gathering of Adeline Sinclair's contributions to the city of Dallas at large and in particular, this park. He pointed out that today would have been her ninety-third birthday, and the crowd responded with applause and cheers. The music swelled and a cloud of multi-colored balloons rose above the stage and floated across the park.

"You okay, babe?" Noah reached out to hug Robyn to his side

"Yes, I'm wonderful. As Adeline would say, it's a glorious day!"

Author's Notes

I just happened onto the mystery of the Tucker & Sherrard revolver. It was one of those tantalizing facts that jumps out when you are searching for something else entirely. There truly was a gun factory in Lancaster, Texas, charged by the Confederate State of Texas to manufacture 3,000 copies of the Colt Dragoon 44 for use by the southern armies. But, the record shows, the story becomes fractured there. Other than a few prototypes, were the guns ever really produced? And if they were, were they shipped? How many were shipped? And finally, what happened to the payment in gold from the Texas Legislature? These are all questions that have been offered up, but never answered.

At the time, though, I was researching something else entirely. I was interested in the story of the La Reunion colony and how its members influenced the tiny settlement of Dallas in the late 1800s. The spot where my research crossed paths with the guns was when Paul Henri, one of the La Reunion colonists, was hired as an engraver by Tucker & Sherrard and eventually came to be left in charge of the company when the Tuckers were accused of treason.

What caught my attention and sparked my imagination was that Paul Henri, a French intellectual, was known to be a strong supporter of the Union and an opponent of slavery. How did he come to be connected with the Confederacy? And, I wondered, if he were, how might he react differently to the task of supplying arms to a cause he did not whole-heartedly support? Many men in the South had to find answers to that question during the Civil War. Most Texans did not own slaves. The issue that caused strife in Texas was states' rights, and many Texans did not totally agree with secession from the United States. Should they flee to Mexico (and many did), or join the Union and fight against their own people, (some did), or should they shelve their personal ideals and step forward to support their homes and communities? Paul Henri seemed to be of the latter group. But could he be the reason the guns have never been found?

The house on Swiss Avenue is a composite of homes, real and imaginary. Only the avenue is there today. It was named for the Swiss La Reunion colonists because it led from the village of Dallas to the farms the colonists started after they left the colony. And, I was happy to find when I visited, the history of the area has been maintained. On one side of Swiss Avenue sets a row of lovely 1800s Victorian houses, some restored, some replicas, surrounded by picket fences that actually do provide office space for a series of nonprofit organizations. Across the street near the area of Swiss and Nussbaumer (he was also a colonist) was the location of Henry Boll's house, although it is no longer standing. In its place is a new meeting hall and collection of offices also for nonprofits. Next to it is, in fact, a park. Sometimes imagination does become real.

Henry Boll, like his friend Paul Henri, was a La Reunion colonist who apparently chose to put aside his aversion to slavery and his belief in the Union of States to join the Confederacy and fight for his new community. In later years after the war, Boll went on to be a prominent citizen in the development of

Dallas. In my imagination I used his home to carry the story forward.

The sense of history found in long-standing houses along the avenue is very intriguing. Houses have personalities picked up in bits and pieces from the events that are played out inside their walls. I created my house from a collection of stories I have gathered in my research over the years.

Adeline and Robyn became my bridge across the century. A study in ways that we are shaped by how we respond to events we encounter. In an effort to find purpose in our personal lives, we make decisions everyday, for good or bad, greed or kindness, love or hate, convenience or conviction that shape each of us. And those choices were my link between the past and the present.

 **IRENE SANDELL** is the author of two award winning novels, *In a Fevered Land* and *River of the Arms of God.* A dedicated historian, she weaves her heart-felt stories around intriguing facts from the past. She also writes, films, and produces documentary films on Texas history. The House on Swiss Avenue is Irene's third novel.